Escape reality with more books from Simon Pulse

Wake
Lisa McMann

Unleashed
Kristopher Reisz

Prama
Jamie Ponti

Crimes of the Sarahs
Kristen Tracy

MY SUMMER ON EARTH

TOM LOMBARDI

SIMON PULSE

NEW YORK LONDON TORONTO SYDNEY

This book is a work of fiction. Any references to historical events, real people, or real locales are used fictitiously. Other names, characters, places, and incidents are the product of the author's imagination, and any resemblance to actual events or locales or persons, living or dead, is entirely coincidental.

SIMON PULSE

An imprint of Simon & Schuster Children's Publishing Division

1230 Avenue of the Americas, New York, NY 10020

Copyright © 2008 by Thomas Lombardi

All rights reserved, including the right of reproduction

in whole or in part in any form.

SIMON PULSE and colophon are

registered trademarks of Simon & Schuster, Inc.

Designed by Mike Rosamilia

The text of this book was set in Filosofia.

Manufactured in the United States of America

First Simon Pulse edition May 2008

2 4 6 8 10 9 7 5 3 1

Library of Congress Control Number 2007937058

ISBN-13: 978-1-4169-5563-4

ISBN-10: 1-4169-5563-1

For Ivana

ACKNOWLEDGMENTS

Alex Glass, who appeared at the lip of the gigantic bucket of failure in which I'd fallen, dropped a rope ladder and asked if I'd like to write a young adult novel. His intelligence, wisdom, encouragement, editorial skills, and kindness have shaped not only this book but my life. Mike del Rosario—without his patience and keen eye for story, I would simply have been lost in space. My homegirls Jennifer Klonsky and Bethany Buck and everyone else at Pulse for giving me a chance. Editors who didn't touch this book but whose words inspired it: John Glassie, Brett Valley, Michelle Orange. Todd Smith's translation. Matthew "Joe" Byrne. Marisol's cooking. Family—Donald, Maureen, Maura, Jim, Paul, Jeff, Ron, Sophie, Nicole, Sarah, and Rachel—who believed in my writing when most had scarcely read a word. Venice Beach, along whose magical sand I was bestowed this idea. And last but not least, the beautiful and lively Ivana, who labored tirelessly over these drafts.

No man can really say that he knows what joy is until he has experienced peace. And without joy there is no life, even if you have a dozen cars, six butlers, a castle, a private chapel and a bomb-proof vault.

—Henry Miller, *The Colossus of Maroussi*

Earth is approaching and I'm breaking apart.

I'm going to evaporate; I just know it. Meanwhile, the spacecraft is rattling so much right now that everything, including my molecules, is beginning to—blink?

Yes, I appear to be vanishing. And then appearing. The craft must have entered another patch of darkness. Either that or I'm passing through a galaxy where all matter and shit . . . just . . . blinks.

Fuck!

Yeah, well, it's . . . great to be traveling at dark-speed.

```
[begin log: 1000.00]
```
Recording log, Father.

Here goes. Am total douche for volunteering to go on this mission. One, scared. Two, dark-speed rearranging my molecules, rearranging my thoughts, making me babble more than usual—and trust me, I like to babble. We used to fly at light-speed. Guess the shit took too long. Question: Why do we need to travel this fucking fast?

Oops.

Not supposed to swear on this thing. Father, you and members of the Central Committee will listen to it. Then again, you're so busy you'll probably order one of your beings to debrief you.

[pause]

Fuck this log!

I don't know, I just feel strange babbling into something Father might listen to. I'd rather babble into nothing. But what if the scientists programmed another log into me, like, a log I don't know about; and Father and them are listening to this right now?

Am excited to walk on the Los Angeles sector of the United States of Earth. I don't know, though . . . states all united? Sounds kind of douchey.

Wait, the craft just disappeared.

Hello?

Hello!!!

[resume log: 930.33]

Per the central committee's orders, I've been sent to Earth to retrieve a being from my planet who's become not only a citizen of Earth but also an "Oscar-nominated actor."

Many earthling years ago, this being of ours embarked on his own mission to Earth to conduct studies on the environment there; only, he *defecated*, and was never heard from again. Heh heh. That was a joke in case any earthlings get a hold of his log. Anyway, he *defected*. Then became so famous that, according to our accounts, youthful earthlings have been pasting his photographs to the walls of their homes. Then, when he began losing popularity among earthlings, check this—this being of ours, I call him the douche—starts constructing a movie and shit about our planet, giving away serious bits of information that potentially pose a threat to our security. We can't have that.

That's where my mission comes in.

Which I'm perfect for, 'cause when we're born, only our parents can sense us. So if a younger being travels to Earth to apprehend the actor, the actor won't sense him.

When I found out they wanted a younger being to embark on a mission to Earth, I begged Father to let me go. He was all, "It's too dangerous." I was all, "I want to do this for the committee." He said my loyalty toward the committee was "impressive." 'Cause he's an important being, he signed me up for the mission and shit.

For as long as I can remember I've always wanted adventure.

3

[pause]
Fuck! What am I saying? This stupid dark-speed is affecting me in strange ways. I just thought I'd, like, turned the log off, but I kept it on. Now Father's going to think I'm giving away information I'm not supposed to. Here comes a dark patch. . . .

[resume log: 910.21]
I wish we spent more time together, Father. There. I feel like a total douche admitting this stuff, but it's the truth. You're always talking about the truth. Well, the truth is, if you took your work for the central committee away you'd probably evaporate. Mother evaporated, like, way before she was meant to evaporate, Father, don't you agree? I have no memory of her. . . .

[pause]

If earthlings somehow get a hold of this log or if they're, like, holding me captive—to study me for technological advances, cut me open and shit?—there are some things they should know.

One, we don't have bodies. We're a mist of electrical waves of molecular activity. Visually, we're a spectacular blend of infinite, glowing colors. If an earthling were to see us I'd guess we'd look like a bunch of dots in the air, you know, depending on how we feel. See, we're always changing shapes and shit. If we get angry, those molecules might expand into gigantic, red cubes. When we cry, it might look like each molecule is breaking apart, falling. . . .

Two, in order for us to assimilate into earthling culture, we have to wear earthling suits. What sucks is that I'm not wearing the suit I'd picked out. Per my instructional, I went through all these images of earthlings, and found a suit that I liked. The scientists said no, can't have it—fuck you. They didn't say it like that, but you know—anyway, I told them I got all relaxed whenever I looked at it, and that I didn't like any of the varieties they chose. You know, I was the one who had to wear the thing. They insisted I choose from their selection, that it was for my "own benefit." As for their selections, some looked lonely, some angry, some sad, some untrustworthy, some untrustworthy and lonely. I said I wanted to arrive looking like an earthling, not a doucheling. When they said nothing, I remembered these beings were afraid to say no to Father. So were they afraid to say no to me now too?

Whatever. I slipped into the suit I'd wanted—it felt incredible! In fact, using the earthling hands portion of the suit, I felt it up and down for such a long time they had to take it away from me. It had these soft, cushiony portions below the neck area. And I was all feeling around between its legs when Father appeared in the room. As usual, he didn't ask how I'm doing, if I'm scared about the mission and shit. No, he just appeared in the shape of a square—which means he's a little disappointed. Anyway, he was all, "Son, why are you hindering the mission?"

"Father, I'm sorry, but I can't stop feeling the suit."

"The suit is of the female variety," said the scientist.

Father was all, "I'm not sure if you are ready." Then we totally shared this moment together where, like, maybe he actually imagined me evaporating, 'cause for the first time ever it felt like I had an advantage over him. But instead of enjoying it, I felt bad, and wanted to give this power back. Then I was all mad at myself for feeling this way. So I said I was sorry for wanting to wear the female earthling suit.

The scientists then quickly programmed me with a "basic gender instructional." Moments later, I was understanding the "basic nature" of sex on Earth; how every earthling wants to make love with a fellow earthling, like, all the time; that making love is more important than almost anything on Earth. They make it all over the planet—in their homes, in parks, in "alleyways," in cars, in "hotels," in bathrooms. . . . Apparently, earthling love makes them feel all alive. So to myself, I was all, I can't wait to get some of this shit!

Love on our planet, you know, is very different. For one, our beings have transcended sex, which is to say, we, like, no longer engage in it. We use technology to procreate—and even that's rare. After many generations of disease and shit, we have figured out ways to control population down. Now we have no disease. Producing offspring is a rare event for which all kids of committees and authorizations and formal ceremonies and boring shit are involved. According to one instructional, on Earth it's easier to, like, get approved for a vehicle purchase than it is to have a little earthling. It makes me sad for my planet. So one, I'll probably never have a family. Two, will never have sex. And three, I don't know . . . maybe best not to focus on it?

Anyway, after Father vanished and we all relaxed again—he can make everyone tense—I was all, to the scientists, "How about injecting me with the love instructional?"

"Your father wanted to know if we could somehow censor your curses."

"Fuck that," I said. When they got all quiet I said, "Oh, I'm just kidding—no, seriously, what about this making of the love instructional?"

"We're afraid we cannot."

"I won't tell Father."

"We've tried to develop it several times, but it's—"

"Beyond logical comprehension."

"But I thought earthlings weren't as advanced as us?"

"Love holds no physical or determinable or discernable value on Earth."

"There's no knowledge with which to equip you."

"Really?"

"Love has nothing to do with the focus of your mission."

"So what if I come across it, and don't, like, recognize it—and it harms me?"

"Your suit will protect you."

"What the fuck is that supposed to mean?"

"Shall we ask your father?"

"I'm sorry."

"He's right, without a love instructional, he's doomed."

"He's not doomed."

"I'm doomed?"

"Let's discuss his earthling suit."

The suit looked more like a rendition of an earthling than an actual earthling. So I was all, "I can't go down there looking like that! It looks fake. . . ."

"Let's see what your father—"

"All right, all right, enough about Father. I'll do it."

"According to our analysis," one scientist said excitedly, his molecules expanding and shit, "actor types, such as the being in question who defected, and now the central focus of your mission, are highly regarded in the Los Angeles sector of California, which happens to be a focal point of the beginning and end of your mission. We have designed your earthling suit after an altogether different, but nevertheless very prominent and successful actor who has appeared in several films on Earth, many of which have won him an array of awards. Earthlings, in many cases, regard these films and their actors more highly than their governing leaders. We have reason to believe, therefore, that the actor after whom we have designed your suit is respected by the majority on Earth as an intelligent, confident, and competent earthling—"

"So as to avoid creating a mere replica," the other scientist interrupted, all drifting in circles all of a sudden, "we've designed the suit to resemble a younger version of this prominent actor."

"Yeah yeah yeah," I said, 'cause I couldn't think of anything else to say.

Then Father appeared in the room again. "Maybe you're not ready to embark on this mission."

"I'll wear the suit," I said, suddenly desperate to travel far away from my planet.

"It's for your own good."

"You don't get me, Father."

Of course, by the time I finished saying this, he vanished.

"There's another area of concern," said one of the scientists. "If we give you all the necessary instructionals, there's a risk of program overload, which would invariably cause confusion that would not only hinder your mission, but possibly pose grave danger to yourself."

"Precisely. So you have a choice," the other one said. "Either get them all at once, or only a selected, vital few."

I was all, wanting to leave for Earth already, "Selected vital—whatever."

"You'll have to learn various lessons of life on Earth on your own."

"How fucking hard can it be?"

"Language."

"Sorry."

"We also have an earthling name for you," said one of them, his molecules forming blue spheres as he got all excited, "according to a recent name search we culled together by conducting years of research, your name—"

"Your name shall be Stanley L. Boriswat."

"Oh come on, that's, like, total douchey—no way!"

"He cannot contest the chosen name."

"You may not contest the chosen name."

"What's the name of the actor the suit's designed after then?"

"Clint Eastwood."

I thought about this for a moment and said, "Not bad."

"You cannot use his name," one of them said, "it will compromise your identity and the entire mission."

"Clint Eastwood—yeah, I like it."

"Stanley L. Boriswat," the other said, "that's your name."

They vanished from the room.

"Idiots," I said.

"We heard that!" one of them shouted from another sector.

"I'm not going to be Stanley Borisdouche or whatever his name is."

"Boriswat!" the other shouted.

In case any earthlings are all listening and shit, and wondering if we've sent other beings on missions to Earth, a few have evaporated. Well, except for one who became an actor. Oh, yeah—we have a switch that can turn off Earth's sun anytime we please. We did it once. Remember the Ice Age? Heh heh. Kidding.

"PRIMARY DESCENT ENGAGED."

What the . . .

[resume log: 200.13]

"FIRST-STAGE LANDING ENGAGED"

Thought: I'm not a mission kind of being. Question: Is it too late to send someone else?

"SECOND-STAGE DESCENT ENGAGED."
This is not supposed to—
"FINAL-STAGE LANDING ENGAGED."
Help!!!

3

[resume log: 50.00]

Ejected from craft.

Hurtling toward "shore."

Thought: Earth does not want me.

The sky looks so completely different from the images on the instructional. A strange blue dotted with—

Yanked underwater. All is black.

Please . . .

Help.

[49.90]

Am ascending into the air again, staring at a gigantic cloud that, against the sky, is the whitest thing ever seen.

Earthling suit made of a material that's supposedly impenetrable to any weapon or substance on Earth. Based on one instructional about earthling wars, pretty sure some earthlings would give their heads for this material. That's all cool, but am hoping suit will withstand gravity and not let me float off into space like a total douche. . . .

Penetrating ocean again. Spinning around in the darkness.

Thought: Do not like the dark.

[pause]

Per the mission, I'm meant to arrive in the Los Angeles sector of California. Ascending into the air again, I find myself forgetting about sectors altogether and, like, completely in awe over this gigantic cloud, its white edges against the blue sky for some reason relaxing my molecules . . . until I'm spinning underwater in the darkness, questioning, once again, as I tumble into the depths of the angry water, if Father was right, that I'm not ready for this mission.

Fuck it. I'll just abort. Return to my planet. And forget about this mission altogether.

But something has changed.

One, am no longer in water. Two, earthling with yellow hair is standing over me and pulling at the arm portion of my earthling suit like he wants to remove it, and saying, "Whoa—did you almost drown, brother?"

A wave rises up behind him and then crashes, the water all sliding along the sand and swallowing me along with his feet. I'm so happy I survived the trip I want to, like, express gratitude toward this friendly being from planet Earth.

So I manage to stand up.

Then I find myself lying down again, sand all entering the mouth portion of my suit.

Meanwhile, the earthling with the long, yellow hair is staring at me. Now, according to one instructional, *You can see inside earthlings so as to get a sense of what they're currently feeling or experiencing.* So I'm all looking at this earthling when I notice he's got a toxic substance moving through his body, red bubbles forming a puddle in his stomach area. Now, according to another instructional, *More disease exists on Earth than any planet in the universe.* Maybe this toxic substance is some form of medicine?

He's all, in a real soft voice, "Are you all right, brother?"

What sucks is that if I speak in my language, he'll die—'cause of the high-pitched frequency of our language. If an earthling hears it, his brain will melt or some shit. So I'm all staring at him, afraid to speak.

"You're breathing—that's a start."

The scientists programmed a colloquilator into me in order to translate my thoughts into earthling speech. Time for a test. I'm all, real quietly, hoping he won't die, "I . . ."

"Yeah?" he says, a smile curling across his face. "You what, man?"

"It works," I'm shouting, "it works!"

"I think what you got is a concussion, man. Sometimes they can feel far-out—when I was a kid I fell off a deck and hit my head and next thing I know I'm lying in the hospital feeling like some motherfucker had tried to make an omelet out of my brain."

He smiles, the skin all blue around his eyes. "You okay or what, man?"

I get up again, only this time the air knocks me down. This earthling then grabs the arm portion of my earthling suit and suddenly I'm standing, thinking that the gravity is strong. Now I'm staring at the sand stuck to the black shoes portion of my suit when this earthling's all, "Listen, man, I don't mean to be forward, but—you got any more left on you?"

"More left?"

"You know, man . . . your shit?"

"My shit?"

"You have lots of sand in your mouth," he says, rattling and smiling. I watch him rattle when I realize he was doing what's known as "laughing."

"Your drugs, man—whatever. You packin' or not?"

Drugs! Per my drug instructional, I'm all, "I will not partake in any activity involving drugs. It is against my beliefs." I stick the finger portion of my suit into the mouth portion, clear out some sand, and say it again. He touches his nose like it hurts him, and is all, "Beliefs are for politicians, man."

"Are you my friend?" I ask, 'cause I have no idea what friends are like on Earth. And he smiles and is all, "Hell yeah, I'm your friend, brother. Why not?"

Then he's all staring at me, yellow bubbles now expanding inside him, "Hey man, you look familiar as a motherfucker—you been on TV? You, like, one of them child actors and shit?"

[resume log: 49.54]
Earthling with yellow hair named Kip. Held on to me as I made first steps. Question: Will he die from these toxins?

Per mission, am asking if he knows where bank machine is.

"You kidding me, man?" he says. "I was a bank-robbin' mother-fucker in my former life."

About to ask about this "former life" when I notice in the distance a gigantic "wheel" spinning on what looks like a really big, wooden platform. Am all, raising hand portion toward wheel, "Kip—what the fuck is that?"

"Damn, brother, you must really have gotten your head clocked. It's the Santa Monica Pier."

Earthling males and females lying on sand in hardly any clothing. Little earthling with brown skin runs into ocean. Ocean swallows him. No one seems to care.

We move away from crashing waves; move toward the earthly buildings.

Earthlings traveling along a smooth, black, narrow surface, some of them attached to wheeled vehicles. Pavement. Loving the colloquilator. There's a bicycle. There's a skateboard. A building. A fire hydrant. A cigarette!

Earthlings never stop moving, Father.

"This way," says Kip, pointing toward a building.

Something so raw about the Earth, Father. Palm trees wave. Buildings stand. Ocean crashes. Aircrafts scream overhead. Birds dive into the ocean. Earthlings laugh, talk, walk, smile, shout, yell, converse on electronic devices. Incredible! Everything alive! Earth, Father, is this gigantic organism that just beats and beats and beat . . . am expanding inside the suit.

On one building there is a . . . "Mirror," I say, suddenly looking at the suit while Kip all touches his hair. "I need a fucking haircut—Jesus. I look sixty, brother." Compared to Kip I look . . . fake. "Not to sound like a homo, man, but you got really nice skin. I need to start moisturizing."

Thought: Earthlings will spot me.

"I'm getting depressed staring at myself," Kip says. "Let's bounce, brother."

"Bounce?"

"Let's motor, man. Come on!"

Earthlings walking past us breaking down; bodies filled with anxiety, sadness, pain, nervousness, confusion, depression, fear—mostly fear.

Question: Have I arrived at a strange segment of Earth, like, where earthlings come to get cured for their fears?

Kip is all, "This way, man." Per the bank instructionals, it says "ATM" on machine. Making sure he can't see, I remove nose hair from suit and insert nose hair into bank machine. Machine makes strange noise, then begins dispensing "cash."

Kip's using his knees to stand, laughing. Said something in my own language. Question: Did I kill him? Am all, "Kip! Are you okay—Kip! Are you alive?"

"Nah, man. I'm just happy I met you, is all."

Gave Kip most of the money. Strange smile curling across his face, eyes expanding. That yellow liquid inside him turns red, bubbles expanding.

Kip runs away, disappearing around the corner of the building. I'm all, "Kip!"

First earthling friend.

Gone.

[pause]

Fifty cycles to complete mission before craft dissolves and disappears forever and then I'm stuck on Earth.

Have returned to the same spot on the beach where I met Kip; this way, you know, he'll know where to find me. I guess I'm beginning to feel pretty alone. Meanwhile, the gigantic sun has begun to sink into the endless blue water.

Earth is fucking huge. My planet is tiny.

I will never give away secrets, but I want to tell Kip about our planet, how, like, our galaxy is made up of several, much smaller suns. And, like, instead of orbiting around one, we sort of maneuver between them; how it creates crazy weather patterns, and there are some months where we aren't allowed to travel aboveground. Here, the weather is actually kind of soothing.

Meanwhile, earthlings, some of them wearing small amounts of clothing, pass by me, but I'm afraid to look at them, like maybe they'll know I'm wearing an earthling suit. In fact, I'm thinking I'll never move from this spot on the sand when I see his long, yellow hair coming toward me. I'm all, expanding inside the suit, "Kip!!!"

"You sure you ain't been in the movies, man?" he says and sits down. The toxic substance has bubbled throughout his entire body now. He seems relaxed. Strange.

"No, Kip."

"TV?"

"No, Kip."

"Documentaries?"

"Like . . . documents, Kip?"

"Kind of, man. Only"—Kip waves his hands in front of his face—"moving."

"Moving documents?"

"Hey, that's a far-out way of putting it."

Meanwhile, the sun has disappeared behind a cloud and the ocean has gone all dark from the lack of light. Now I'm thinking the water had disappeared and we'll get swallowed up in all the darkness. There's this planet in our galaxy that has developed these huge holes that sometimes are there and sometimes are not; their beings can get swallowed into these without warning. I want to tell Kip about this.

"I know you're an actor, man," Kip says, opening up what I think is a canister. "I used to be an actor, brother."

"Like, an Oscar-nominated actor?"

"Let me tell you something about the acting world. Everyone is fake—even the moms, man. It's true. The thing of it is, man, the thing is . . . is that I used to think it was L.A., but it's not. It's capitalism, man. The government spreads so much greed around this country that people have no choice but to act disingenuous and shit. You know, cats are protecting their money, man. They have to. It's the wild kingdom. Nothing's changed. We're just a bunch of apes with iPods now, man. You know?"

I don't entirely get what he's saying, so I just smile douche like and listen.

"The thing of it is, man, is that it's a ginormous salad bowl of fakeness, with croutons and cucumbers. Fresh pepper and shit like that. I've worked in restaurants, man. The government is the chef, man. I know. Hey, take a young handsome man like yourself. You got a face they want, man. You're a ripe avocado. I'm twenty-five pushing sixty. No one wants me. People are dying all over the world 'cause of greed, man. Sleep on the beach, you'll start to see it. No appointments, no disappointments. These rich fuckers . . . they ain't happy. But you're an exception to the rule, a good soul, I can tell. Hey, by the way, don't mean to pry, brother, but where'd you get all this loot? You been in some big movies or commercials or shit?"

Before I can respond, Kip's all, "Yep—usually how the shit works. Hey, what's your name, brother?"

"Clint."

"Oh that's cool, man."

"Clint Eastwood."

Kip claws at the sand. "Clint fuckin' Eastwood. Why not?"

Kip pulls a canister from a bag and is all, "Got you a beer for your troubles, Mr. Eastwood." He then pours the liquid down his mouth, and I'm wondering if the beer helps sooth the toxins inside him. I watch him consume the liquid. Then I lean back and pour the beer down the mouth portion of my suit. Per its design, the liquid disintegrates inside.

"Right on," Kip says, "guess you don't like to savor but that's cool, man."

Meanwhile, the ocean's going black, the sky gray, and I'm contracting to the lower stomach portion of the suit. Kip is all, "You smell something burning, man?"

The beer disintegrating in the suit produces a smell, but I don't think I've been programmed to smell. Per my instructional, I say what I'm supposed to say whenever I take food or drink into the suit. "It must be the kitchen."

"Must be the kitchen," Kip laughs and slaps his thigh, "I like that. Clint fuckin' Eastwood. Far-out motherfucker."

I'm about to ask Kip about his toxins when he's all, "Know something, your mouth moves funny when you talk." All of a sudden his eyes, like, start to close, and he falls slowly back onto the sand.

Earthlings—one moment they're talking the next they're sleeping . . . wait, what did he say about my mouth? Oh, no! The douchey scientists, they screwed something up! Maybe the colloquilator was not responding, like, directly with my mouth. I can't go on like this. Wait, per my instructional, I have to make sure I landed in the right sector. I'm all, covering my mouth now when I talk, "Kip, where am I?"

"Venice Beach, man—home of the homefree."

"Wait, is this, like, the Los Angeles sector?"

Kip smiles, his eyes still closed. "Yep. Sector. I like that shit. Sector."

At least the douchey scientists landed me in the right sector. Suddenly, this pink light fills the massive, graying space where the ocean meets the sky, and I'm getting the sensation the mission will change me forever when, like, this female voice says, "You know that you have money falling out of your pocket?"

Pocket. There must be glitches in the colloquilator! Per one of the instructionals, I'm programmed, whenever confused by earthling-speak, to just thank them.

"Thanks," I say.

This earthling standing over me has hair the color of peanut butter, which is apparently a substance females her age enjoy. Perhaps she, like, rubbed this substance in her hair. I'm all, "I like the peanut butter in your hair."

She laughs. In fact, she laughs so hard I worry she might die. Then she's all shoving her earthling hand into the slits in my earthling pants, and just before she finishes, I shout, "Pocket— that's what it is!"

"God," she says, "you're, like, on some wacky shit, huh?"

I'm all, "Thanks."

Wait, what if this earthling suspects I'm wearing a suit? One, she's not filled with toxins. Two, she seems smarter than Kip. The scientists have been monitoring earthling cellular phones, and

since I'm equivalent to a sixteen-year-old earthling, the colloquilator's been programmed to make me sound like a sixteen-year-
old from the vast land whose states are all united and shit. But how
do I know I'm speaking right? She's all staring at me now, so I'm
all, per my instructional, "I live in the Los Angeles sector of California. I like cashew nuts and my favorite movie is *Jaw*."

"You're stupid funny," she says, taking a seat on the other side
of Kip, so that he's lying between us. "My name's Zoë," she says, all
smiling.

"I like your name."

"Thanks, it means 'life.' What's yours?"

"Stanley," I say, "it means 'douche.' No. That's not my name."

"Wait, why would you, like, tell me the wrong name?"

"It's Clint . . . Clint Eastwood."

"Like, the actor?"

"Yeah but . . . it's—"

"Wait, let me guess, your parents were, like, obsessed with Dirty
Harry?"

Per another instructional, I'm meant to say "sort of" whenever
I'm confused with a question, like's Zoë's next question: "Are your
parents, like, in the film business?"

"I don't know, like . . . sort of."

"I'll bet you grew up with lots of money and nannies and stuff
like that?"

"I don't know, like . . . sort of."

"That's cool."

There's something about her molecules that relaxes me, and I'm thinking I've found earthling love. First a friend, then love—how exciting Earth is so far! I'm all, expanding inside, "What's your, like, purpose on Earth, Zoë?"

"On Earth? Uh, let's see, I don't, like, have a purpose, I'm only fifteen." She looks out at the black waves and then is all, "I guess art is my purpose—yeah, that's like . . . yeah."

"What is art?"

"Oh, God," she says, "that's way too hard to answer without some dumbass teacher around."

"What is God?"

"Wow, you're, like, way philosophical." She puts both her hands into her hair and says, "I like that."

Suddenly, this silver planet appears from behind the clouds, and I'm all, staring at it, "Moon!" Oops, I have to be careful not to yell stuff like that.

Meanwhile, Zoë's hair practically covers her face when she lets go of it. In the now silver light, I see that her face is dotted with these red spots that I find absolutely beautiful. Using a finger portion of the suit, I touch her face and tell her these spots "are pretty and shit."

"Don't!"

"Did I hurt you?"

"You making fun of my zits?"

"Zits?"

"Zits can't be beautiful—I hate them."

"I think they are pretty."

"Know something? You're strange. For sure."

"I am?"

"But sweet," she says, and then begins to eat her finger-nails. Since my fingernails serve as tracking monitors to find the douche's house, I decide against eating them. Meanwhile, inside I see that she is sad and lonely and, most of all, lost; but full of hope. I don't know if I can always tell what each thing looks like—each takes its own shape. Sadness looks like what earthlings might call a "pond," I think. Inside Zoë is this silver pond that, judging by its shape, may have been around for a long time. Hope, I'm thinking, is this jagged streak of light . . . she has one, it's small, but growing. Slowly.

I'm all, thinking of what she asked earlier, "Did you, like, grow up with lots of parents and a nanny and stuff?"

"Lots of parents?" She laughs. "You're hilarious." Then she gets all serious and says, "I'm sort of a runaway."

"Oh," I say, afraid to ask what that means. Wait, according to the colloquilator, a "runway" is *a flat strip of pavement on which aircrafts land.* Which makes no fucking sense. Still, I'm all, "So you're, like, flat pavement that aircrafts land on?"

Inside Zoë's pond turns all green, and she looks at me with this smile taking over her face, her zits all red and pretty. "You crack me up, you know that?"

I just smile at her all douchely, 'cause I don't know what that means.

"I don't know," Zoë's saying, "maybe I'm not a total runaway . . . or a runway, but, like, I'm glad it's summer, 'cause I'm totally not going back to school. I mean, don't get me wrong, I'm not going to end up like one of those annoying kids on the commercials all, like, slathered in the high school dropout vibe, you know? But I just want to take some time off and, like, figure some stuff out. . . . I mean, what's so wrong about that? The teachers at the school are total nothings—am I supposed to want to be like them? But I sleep at my mother's house half the time, so—she's a certified, professional nonentity—and sometimes I sleep with my friends in this camper on the beach. Which is okay. I mean, when it's not smelling like ass or dirty socks. For sure."

I like listening to Zoë speak, although I don't entirely understand everything. Like, what the fuck is "high school dropout vibe?" I don't want to ask her, though, or else she might think that I haven't been listening. Maybe this Zoë, I'm thinking, smiling all douchely at her, can teach me something about earthling love.

Then I'm realizing she doesn't like where she lives, so I'm all, "Zoë, maybe I can buy you a new house."

"Can you?" She laughs.

Now I'm thinking about asking her if we can make some love somewhere when some earthling yells, "Zoë!"

"Oh," she says, all getting up and wiping sand from her clothing, "that's my friend. Hey—see you around, all right?" Inside, I begin to contract, and I'm about to ask what the fuck that's supposed to mean when she's all, "Hey, you want to meet here tomorrow, like, around the same time?"

"Yes!"

"'Kay," she says, "see you then." She's all walking toward the doucheling who'd called her name.

"Kip," I say, but he doesn't wake up. Meanwhile, the ocean moans, its black water all scratching at the sand as it makes its way toward us, wanting, I'm pretty sure, to swallow us whole.

4

Zoë said to meet her "here tomorrow, like, around the same time."
According to the colloquilator, "tomorrow" is *the day follow-ing today*. And "today" is *the present time*. And "time" is *indefinite and continuous duration regarded as that in which events succeed one another*.

Question: When the fuck do I meet her?

Walking away from beach now. Red building blocking sun that's hanging high over the Los Angeles sector. Do not like darkness. Cars roaring. Sunlight appears again after I pass building. Thought: The light turns everything gold.

Two females coming at me along "sidewalk."

Thought: If I'm going to experience earthling love before start-ing mission, why not experience with two at the same time?

One of the females has hair the color of sand; the other's is the color of pavement. Their skin is the same color as their hair. Sandy-skinned. Black-skinned. I am taller in height. When they get close, I'm all, "Hello."

"Hi, there," the sandy one says.

"Strange shoes," the black one says. "But I dig."

"Where'd you get those?" the sandy says. "Around here?"

"I don't know, like . . . sort of."

"Are you French?" the sandy asks.

"No," I say, not entirely sure what this means, "are you?"

Her eyes are the color of the ocean—the other female has eyes the color of Zoë's hair. I'm all, "You both have cool eyes."

"Thanks," the sandy says with a smile.

Am all, suddenly realizing I don't know my own, "Can you tell me what color my eyes are?"

"Hmm," says the black, "gray?"

"Silver, I think—hey, you look familiar."

"You have strange skin," says the black, "it's, like, very unusual looking."

Inside they're filled with these white and orange what looks like fingers, all gripping onto one another. Can't sense what this means, but it appears friendly. Am all, "Can we all go somewhere to make love? You know, it shouldn't take too long. Well, hopefully. 'Cause I have this thing I have to accomplish. Which, you know—I can't talk about."

The black laughs so loud she has to step back, like maybe to hold herself up? The sandy, meanwhile, is suddenly filled with this blinking light behind her eyes. Anger.

"Fucking loser," she says as they both walk away.

"Wait," I ask them, "what did I lose?"

The females keep walking.

A "loser" is, according to the colloquilator, *the opposite of a winner. Winner applies to a competition that ensues between earthlings, usually on a playing field.*

Question: If I'm a loser, how do I become a winner?

[48.61]

One-armed earthling coming at me. Am thinking he lost his arm, 'cause he's all looking around with a nervous face like maybe the earthling who took the arm is nearby. Question: Why would an earthling steal an arm? Unless he got his arm taken from some other earthling.

One-armed is filled with similar toxins as Kip, his veins flowing with that yellow liquid, except in his case the stuff is all bubbling, like it's about to seep out his skin. Am all, "Do you need help finding your arm?"

"No."

"Okay."

"Hey, fuck you."

"Fuck me?"

He scratches at the face portion of his body. "You got any change?"

"Change me?"

"Money—you got any money?"

31

"I have lots of money," I say, reaching into one of the pockets of my pants. When he sees the money, he starts scanning the area like he's worried the earthling who took his arm will now take his money, but this sort of worry must be temporary, 'cause he just snatches it pretty quickly. Meanwhile, am noticing he's got red stuff—blood!—on his fingernails, and the portion of his face he's been scratching is actually open, revealing more blood. Inside he appears to be very sad. I can see so clearly it's like I can reach inside of him and touch this gray puddle the yellow toxins are bubbling into. Thought: Ask where I can ascertain a car for the mission. "Do you know where—"

"You been in the movies or something?"

"No."

"Yeah, you have," he says, all scratching and walking off fast now.

"No, I haven't."

"*Yeah* you have *yeah* you have!"

"Wait," I say, but he just keeps walking away, like, maybe he's knows I'm losing.

Am turning around to see cars flashing past on paved path. "Road," I say, but no one's, like, listening. Thought: Too dangerous to cross.

[48.52]

Standing on sand, waiting for Zoë. Not sure what "around the same time" means. Afraid to start the mission. Sorry, Father, but that's just the truth.

By the way, Father, Zoë is a female earthling whose molecules relax me.

Speaking of molecules, mine are starting to, like, fall . . . am beginning to cry. Don't want to be here anymore, Father.

[48.40]
Like a gigantic piece of "fruit" that I saw a female earthling eating earlier, the sun drops all slow like into the endless rolling blue water.

Four earthling males with no shirts appear to have involved themselves within some sort of thin, blue square that's been marked on the sand. Inside their bodies each is filled with red and blue spheres that vibrate—a kind of energy I can't sense. Rage? One of them holds a "ball." Then makes this ball ascend like a small planet over this strange thing. . . . "Net!" Ah, a competition—how exciting!

Suddenly, one of the males ascends into the air and then strikes a hand against the ball, like he's angry at it, and ball then travels over the net. . . .

Where, like, the other male strikes it with his hand—sending the ball straight up into the air.

Move so close that I can hear one of the males, who's holding the ball, say, "Fives."

Suddenly, his blue and red spheres melt into a kind of orange liquid—confusion—and he's all, "What're you looking at?"

"Are you a loser?" I say, wanting to know what a loser looks like.

"The fuck you just say?"

He's got a blinking light inside his head. Anger. Uh-oh. Am all, "Just wanted to know if you're a loser or a winner."

The ball suddenly smashes against the face portion of my suit, the light in his head blinking so fast it's become a constant.

"You want to get hit again, dumb fuck?"

"No."

"That's what I thought."

I walk toward the water, shrinking inside the suit. Thought: Never speak to douchelings involved on playing field. Only talk to winners. In fact, probably losers don't bother talking to other losers. Makes sense.

Question: Without a net, how do I spot a winner?

[48.22]

Sitting on the beach, Father—a little afraid for some reason to look at earthlings . . . except for females.

Thought: Should probably start mission.

[pause]

Pink particles of light have formed in the gray sky where the sun had dropped. Meanwhile, the water is black, roaring all angrily as it spills out toward me.

I don't like the darkness.

"Same time here," Zoë said. I think she said that. I'm an idiot! One instructional said earthlings make love all over the planet, and I have been down on Earth for a short while and I can't seem to get it.

[resume log: 48.13]

Will have to resume mission without Zoë, without earthling love, without fear. Fear, I'm thinking, is, like, everywhere on Earth. No choice but to start mission.

Bird just deposited what appears to be a toxic substance in my hair. Question: Is that a signal from you, Father—if so, maybe a message with your voice would be better?

[47.90]

A bird is talking to me. Didn't get the instructional on that. The sun has begun rising, filling the sky with what looks like gigantic, purple earthling fingers. Question: How do I speak bird?

"Clint!" the bird says again.

"What?" I say, looking up at the bird, only to see, like, two of them now—one black, one white—flapping in the air, looking down at me. Their eyes are black and empty.

They fly away.

"Losers!" I say.

"Clint!"

I turn to see Zoë walking toward me, with her hands in her pockets. She came back!

Her peanut butter hair flaps all bird like in the wind. I'm so excited I expand into so many parts of the suit at once that I worry my molecules will suddenly blow the arms off. Which, you know, I'm not so sure Zoë would, like, appreciate.

[pause]

"Zoë!" I say, sensing, as she nears, that she's excited to see me. Only, she doesn't seem to act the way she's feeling. Like, inside she's got these green waves of liquid. But she talks like she's bored and shit: "You been here long?" So I'm all, thinking I should also act like she's the last earthling I want to see, "Hey."

And she's all, "Hey."

And we're both talking like we're tired.

"Hey."

"Hey."

"Hey."

"I'll stop when you stop," she says and smiles.

"Hey."

She laughs, then sits down real hard on the sand, something erupting from her buttocks that sounded like . . . maybe she sat on a small animal or something? Strange. Her insides have shrunken into these tiny, red and blue particles. So I'm all, "What is wrong all of a sudden?"

"Oh, like you don't know!"

The waves scratch at the sand, only to retreat and then threaten us again. I'm all, just happy to be sitting with her, "Is it something I did?"

"No."

"Something I said?"

"No."

"Like, what then?"

"Just drop it, Clint!"

While the sun falls, I start wondering if this is why the douche stayed behind—beautiful earthling love.

"I farted," Zoë says.

"A fart," I say, allowing the colloquilator to do the rest, "'is flatus expelled through the anus.'"

"I guess," she says, and then is all, "Oh my God, I'm, like, so embarrassed—I can't believe I just told you that!"

"Why embarrassed?"

"Come on, Clint, like you don't do it."

"I probably do," I say, not knowing what to say.

She stares at me, and then says, "Boy . . . you're an odd bird."

"Do I look like a bird?"

"No." She laughs. "It's just . . . you know, I've never told that to a boy before."

"That he's a bird?"

"No, idiot! That I"—she all lowers her voice—"farted."

She leans onto the shoulder portion of my suit. We look like other male and female earthlings sitting on the sand, all close and shit, so I'm all, "Zoë . . ."

"Clint, speaking of birds, I think you have, like, bird shit in your hair."

"I do?"

"When was the last time you showered?"

"Uh . . ."

"I just didn't realize you were living on the beach."

"Like Kip."

"Yeah, like Kip and lots of people."

"Zoë?"

"Yeah?"

"Can we go make love in a bathroom?"

She smiles, then lies back on the sand, and looks at me all seriously now and shit, "Fresh."

"Fresh?"

"That's what my mom used to say to my dad when he used to make, like, you know, fresh jokes. I don't know, fresh. What does it mean?"

"I don't like questions."

"You know something, Clint. Your mouth moves funny when you talk. Or like—you talk out the side of it, I think."

"It does?"

"Wait, I didn't mean to offend you."

Then she's all touching the arm portion of my suit and saying, "Man, you're pretty fit."

"What the fuck is that supposed to mean?"

"Relax, it's not like I said you were gay or something."

According to the colloquilator, "gay" is *an earthling who engages in same sex*. As, like, opposed to different sex? Wait, maybe it means sex with the same person, like, forever. "Wait," I say to Zoë, and she's all, "Yeah?"

"Isn't everyone, like, you know, gay?"

Zoë takes in a deep breath, and then is all, "Hmm . . . that's a line from a Nirvana song. You're a deep thinker, Clint."

"Thanks."

"By the way, I'm sorry I didn't meet you on the beach last night. I had to deal with my mom. We, like, totally got in a fight, so I slept in my friend's camper. But I woke up and couldn't sleep for shit. It was kind of gross."

"That's cool," I say, wondering if she'll think I'm a douche if I tell her that her molecules relax me.

Meanwhile, the wind coming off the great big ocean is strong. Now I'm thinking about what she'd said about my mouth and how it moves. Like, what else about my suit did the douchey scientists mess up? Do I walk all strange and shit? I can't identify smell—so what if I smell? All's I can do, I think, is question shit. Whatever.

I wish I could "fart" like Zoë, just to, you know, pretend I'm of this planet. Before I know it I'm touching Zoë's hair, moving it out of the way so I can see her pretty zits—like the way I saw some douche on the beach do it to his female earthling companion. I only call him a douche 'cause, like, after he did that, he got down on his hands and began pushing himself away from the Earth, and then lowering himself, and then repeating this over and over while his female just sort of watched the ocean, like, not really caring about what he was doing. You know, just a douchey thing to do.

Meanwhile, I'm sensing she's troubled inside, this little silver pond she has . . . so I'm all, "I sense you are troubled."

"You're perceptive, Clint. Yeah—I just found out today that my dumbass dad's back in jail. That's what my mom and I were fighting about. She was feeling bad for him. And I was all, like, saying he deserves jail at this point. For sure."

"Where criminals go," I say, loving the colloquilator again, "I know the place."

"It's like, hello, Dad, way to be such a fucking loser."

I want to talk about this word—"loser." You know, if her father is a loser, then what's a winning father look like? Like how's Zoë's father—a loser—ever going to win if, you know, he's just a loser? If he wins once, does he become a winner all of a sudden, or just a loser who won once?

I don't want to interrupt Zoë's thoughts, which I can see inside her head are flashing in streaks of black and yellow. I'm all, "Was he ever a winner?"

"Uh, he's been in jail, like, three times already. I think that makes him a certifiable loser."

"Maybe he, like, isn't good at winning."

"Winning what?"

"I don't know."

"Whatever! Loser. Winner. He's a nothing."

"Maybe douche is a better word."

"More like a deadbeat dad."

"Or a douchebeat dad."

Zoë's body shakes when it laughs, and I find my earthling suit all rattling. I didn't know laughing was part of the suit—it's a strange sensation. Inside I'm vibrating with such joy all of a sudden I wish she would see it.

"You laugh funny," Zoë says.

"Fuck!"

"No, it's cute," she says. "God, Clint, you're kind of intense. Most people I know are, like, checked out. It's cool."

I see that she is fond of me all of a sudden—her body filled with what looks like a green tongue. "Tell me about this douche-beat dad."

"Like you care."

"I do!"

"Oh, God. . . . Okay, he drank. A lot. But the weird thing is when he drank he was cool, or at least nice, funny and stuff, you know? When he wasn't drunk, he'd be all aggro—and would just fight with my mom. Who, like, made everything worse—constantly raggin' on him and stuff. Like, they fought day and night, it was . . . okay, like, my mom used to clean for this theater for two weeks before she got fired. What else is new? Anyway, I used to go with her after school and just stare at this empty stage while she worked, you know? So I guess I started thinking of my parents like they were onstage . . . maybe 'cause they were, like, so predictable? Anyway, I began to think that I was forced to sit in the audience and watch, you know? So when it got to the point when my dad first went to jail, I was, like, happy. 'Cause their dumb show, like, ended. But without my dad, you know, like, without her costar, my mom just sat around doodling all day. Then I became obsessed with her, and I started . . . anyway—now I can't decide who's worse, my mom, who does nothing, or my dad, who drinks. When he lived with us, he came home around the same time at four in the morning—and I'd hear his boots on the carpet. Hear him opening cabinets and stuff . . . then my mom getting all angry and screaming at him . . . so after he went to jail, I just, like, left, I guess."

I grab the back of her head like I saw this one doucheling do and then bring her closer to the face of my suit. I then press her lips against mine.

"Ouch," Zoë says.

"What?"

"I got shocked—weird."

"Sorry."

"It's okay." Then she smiles, squeezes my hand portion, and says, "You're a strange bird, you know that?"

So I try and make a sound like a bird, but it comes out all douchey, and Zoë laughs. Then stops laughing. This time she brings her lips close to mine, only she inserts her tongue into my suit, like she wants me to eat it. I'm all contracting inside the suit so that I don't shock her. And she's all rubbing her tongue around the tongue in my suit and inside my molecules begin to quiver.

[pause]

I take Zoë to the bank machine and remove all its money, even though one instructional programmed me, like, specifically not to do this. Suddenly these red tongues erupt inside Zoë when she sees the cash. Weird, it's like she's attracted to it. And, just like on the beach when she saw me, she acts all cool and shit, pretending she doesn't care. Anyway, buying a house proves to be, in Zoë's words, "a total, like, absolute major pain in, like, the *ass*." So we do supposedly what lots of earthlings do: we rent. We find this blue, wooden house close to the beach, with all kinds of "furniture," and white things called "chaise lounges" on the roof for beings to sit in and stare at the toxic sun. The earthling called "the landlord" tells us we have to sign all these papers. So Zoë says, "We'll just give you all cash." Pink tongues erupt inside the landlord when I show him the money. He says we can rent "month to month," but that an "adult" has to sign some papers. Zoë says we should get Kip.

After Kip signs the papers, he's all, "Where you been all my life, man?" Then asks for more money; only to return later dressed in what looks like clothing he stole from a very large earthling and, with beer in a bag, he's all, "Where you been all my life, man?" I'm all, "You already asked that, Kip." Kip's all, sitting down on the furniture and opening a beer, "Stop the record stop the record stop . . ." He then points a plastic device at the television, and the screen turns on.

I'm amazed by how, like, free of questions Kip seems. Meanwhile, Zoë's talking about what we should do with this "disgusting, like, totally assed-out chair," and Kip's asking where "they keep the ashtrays in this motherfucker." I can't stop looking at the screen of the television: On it, this earthling stands in the back of a roof-free car, holding a gun the size of a small palm tree. He's pointing it at earthlings on the street, this loud noise dispensing from the gun; the earthlings, meanwhile, when they get hit by the bullets, fall to the pavement. Now, according to an instructional, *Guns kill earthlings—stay away from them!* Why, though, this earthling is killing other earthlings does *not* make sense. Maybe the answer will appear. Meanwhile, the earthling with the gun is now laughing as he shoots his fellow earthlings. Kip is laughing too. Then the laughing earthling inside the TV suddenly loses control of the roof-free car and drives into a gigantic glass window.

"Oh, shit!" Kip says all seriously—only to resume laughing.

Glass, like, splashes all over the pavement.

Wait, maybe he felt bad for killing all the earthlings, so he killed himself; and thought it funny that, like, after all that effort to shoot these earthlings, he'd end up killing himself. Meanwhile, the glass has stopped spilling onto the pavement. All's quiet. I'm thinking this earthling learned his lesson when he emerges from the building, glass and blood all over his body and, get this—points the gun at somebeing, and starts smiling.

Wait, why didn't the earthlings, who're now being shot again, run away when they saw other earthlings getting shot? When this douche decides he's had enough, he just walks down the street carrying the gun on his shoulder portion—all, like, satisfied with his work.

The television then turns black. Before I get a chance to ask Kip what's going on, this, you know, female earthling now appears on the TV, showing her baby to us, like, in case we want to get to know it or something; then places the tiny earthling onto a bed. Of course, now I'm wondering if the earthling with the palm tree of a gun is going to enter the room and shoot them. In fact, I'm suddenly curious to see what it looks like when an earthling dies. The screen, meanwhile, gives up on the mother and baby earthling, like maybe they're too boring?—and shows this big blue bottle, and then the words "Johnson & Johnson" come on the screen and . . .

I walk to the window and look outside, just to make sure there's no earthling with a gun shooting earthlings on the street. All is quiet out there. And dark. I don't like the dark, which I want to tell Kip, but something tells me he'd just laugh.

I'm staring out the window when something strikes the head portion of my suit.

"I'm sorry, man," Kip says, "I thought you were looking at me."

"What hit me, Kip?"

"A beer can—you all right, brother?"

"I'm fine, Kip."

"You're indestructible."

"Thanks."

"Drink up, there isn't much time."

"Wait—what do you mean?"

"Just yankin' your chain, man."

I find myself expanding inside the suit and saying, "Don't throw things at me, Kip. I don't like that."

"I'm sorry, brother."

Black, like, hair takes over the inside of Kip's body; which, I think, is shame. Meanwhile, he's pointing that device at the television again, making it change images. One of the images shows earthlings in sand-colored suits shooting guns, only their guns appear smaller than the last gun-shooting earthling.

"Fucking war is a downer, man," Kip says, and inside I see now the black hairs have been replaced by alcohol, or what looks like red liquid forming in what appears to be blue sand or something, this light blinking behind his eyes. So much color moving through him I can't stop looking at him. "What?" he says.

Anyway, according to an instructional, "war" is *a contest carried on by a force of weapons that inevitably results in the murder of numerous earthlings.* So I ask Kip who exactly is forming this war.

"Us, man."

"Us, you mean . . . you and me?"

"Clint fuckin' Eastwood, you're a philosophical motherfucker. Tell me something, man, your rich daddy send you traveling abroad?"

"I don't know, like . . . sort of."

"Mommy and Daddy got the money to send you away but not tell you what's going on?"

"I don't know, like . . . sort of."

"Don't worry—I'll educate you, brother. Heh. Okay, where was I? Oh. The United States of America is at war, and it's—okay, so picture the war as like a big, clogged colon the size of a tunnel. With no fiber in sight, got that, Clint fuckin' Eastwood?"

"Yes, Kip."

"Now, it's going to take an enema the size of the Washington Monument to clear out the mess. And some major fuckin' roughage, man. But I'll tell you what's scary, when that shit gets cleared out . . . it's going to be one unruly mother. Each war is just a bucket of tar, man. Paving the way for capitalism . . . but you know something, man, between you and me, I don't give two shits. Wait a second there, brother, that's like a double entendre or something, what's it called? Drink up—that's what I say. And be merry, man. But you already know this, you're just yankin' my chain. You're a rich, smart cat. This much I know . . . 'cause a little birdie . . . he told me so."

I can't tell if Kip speaks the truth or if he just babbles what, like, pleases him at the moment. Meanwhile, I'm finding myself going to the window again, this time looking for sand-colored suited earthlings shooting other earthlings on the street. Nothing but an earthling with no hair moving past the window on a bicycle. I'm all, "Kip, there's, like, no war out there."

He opens another beer can, looking at me now with his eyes all shut. "Now that's some far-out shit, man. See, I forget we're at war at the moment, and . . . look around, man, and all you see is a bunch of fuckers eatin' ice cream and sippin' ten-dollar lattes and sucking their own dicks on their Rollerblades on the board-walk. Well, they're not doing that, per se, man, but—hey what was I saying?

"Oh, yeah—you can't change the world, Clint fuckin' Eastwood, only yourself."

"The war is where again?" I say, trying to, like, understand.

"Ain't we at war with two countries? Believe it or not, I read the paper sometimes, brother, and let me tell you, sometimes that fucking paper reads me." Kip's laughing while I'm all contracting inside.

"Come on, man—don't get all depressed on me. Know something, my father got all depressed on me once and you know what I did?"

"What, Kip?"

"I shot the sonofabitch."

"You did?"

"No, I'm just yankin' your chain again. The thing of it is, man, is . . . ain't nothing we can do about war, it's USA. Just pay taxes and ride the waves to freedom, man. If you're stupid enough to pay taxes and shit."

"You mean, the vast land whose states are united?"

Kip laughs all loud and says, "I like your style, brother. Rentin' me a house and shit. You're all right."

Zoë comes running down the stairs and is all, "That bed up there is, like, totally freakin' amazing! I laid in it for, like, five minutes and felt like a queen. Clint, get up here. You *have* to, like, experience this."

Kip is all, putting a hand over his mouth, "Let me sniff your fingers later, brother."

And I'm all, "What?" Zoë's all, "You're a disgusting pig, Kip!" He's all, "I'm sorry, man, it's just . . . I'm sorry." She's all, "Don't call me 'man,' Kip, I have a freaking name."

"Sorry, man, won't happen again!" Kip's all laughing, his face turning red as Zoë runs up the stairs.

Then she's running back down and is all, "You know, we just used you for the signing of the lease, Kip. This is a home now. Don't poison the place with your drunken psychobabble!"

Kip suddenly fills with a thick gray liquid-like stuff, these black bubbles floating throughout. "You kicking me out?"

"I didn't say that!"

"If you're kicking me out, just *fucking* say it, man! 'Cause it ain't the first time. Otherwise, if you're not kicking me out, I promise to be the best tenant up in this motherfucker. I will shine your shoes, I will wash your dishes, I will buy toothpaste and tampons and—"

"Enough!" Zoë's running up the stairs again, only this time shouting. "Just, like, respect me, Kip, okay?"

"Yes, ma'am," Kip says.

Then he's all, moving his yellow hair from his face, "Know something, brother, I think the only shot of me ever gettin' some pussy these days is if I grow my own."

I have no idea what he's saying, and when I don't, like, respond, he's all, "I was thinking today, man, I'd like to get me one of them volleyball babes I see on the beach, you know? Saw one today with, like, *pillars* for thighs, man . . . and an ass way up in the air— something I can climb onto, you know, man? Like a monument or some shit I can worship. You're too young to probably—hey, you catchin' my drift or what, man?"

"I don't know, like . . . sort of. "

"Clint fuckin' Eastwood," he's saying, his head starting to fall onto his chest, "I mean no disrespect to your girl up there. Just for record's sake, she's way younger than my type. I'm into older women now that we've gone off record, man. The thought of a woman makes my heart just break into tears, man. The thought of, like, one sittin' on my face . . . no, man! Forget I said that. Really, though, the thought of an older woman . . . not Grandma or any- thing, but I think they call them a cougar, man. Give me a cougar with a heart and I'll give you . . . I'm dying, brother."

"'Cause of your, like, disease?"

"Disease?"

"You don't have one?"

"Only disease I got is a constant cravin' for cougar pussy. Although more I think of it, cougar's kind of a gay term."

"It is?"

"Brother," he manages to say all tired, his eyes closed, "you know it says gullible up on the ceiling there?"

When I look up and don't see any word I'm all, "It doesn't say anything on the ceiling, Kip."

"You're way too easy."

I'm all, suddenly thinking of what he'd said earlier, "Wait—my girl?"

"Ain't you and Zoë an item?"

"I don't know, like . . . sort of."

"Clint!" Zoë says from upstairs. "Get up here!"

When I get upstairs, I walk over to the window and look out.

"What're you looking for, Kip?" Zoë says, sitting on the bed with her legs all crossed over each other.

"War."

"What?" She laughs.

"This land whose states are all united is at war."

Zoë falls back on the bed and starts talking to the roof: "I just *love* the way you talk sometimes, Clint. Yeah—war. Totally bites major freaking ass."

"But where is the war?"

"Oh my God. *Totally!*"

Outside, some palm trees wave back and forth in the ocean wind. "No, Zoë," I say, "where is the *war*?"

"Oh, Clinton, you're such a passionate boy."

"I am?"

"Duh. Most guys don't give a bat shit! For sure. Oh my God this bed is, like, totally fucking royal."

"Have you seen war?"

Zoë starts thinking and then is all, "No. Only on TV."

"So war can only be seen on TV?"

"Like, you said you're from Los Angeles but, like . . . what part?"

I think about what Kip said and I'm all, "I have been traveling a lot."

"You're so lucky. Like, where—Europe?"

"I don't know, like . . . sort of."

"Know something, I don't like to pry, 'cause you seem like the kind of guy who comes from, you know, some serious cash, so I don't want to ask questions . . . but, were you raised by some diplomat or something, or some millionaire who grew up around the world?"

"Hey, why is Kip," I find myself saying, "like, mean?"

"Reminds me of my father, he's drunk. Just talks bullcrap all day long, blah blah blah blah blah . . ."

I join Zoë on the bed, and we lie there without talking. I don't like not babbling, though, so I'm all, "Can we make some love now?"

"Gosh, you're totally pushy."

"I am?"

Inside Zoë suddenly expands with black and yellow spots, which I can't recognize. Then she's all, "I'm sorry, I'm just kind of tired— I kind of just want to sleep, do you mind?"

"Wait—you're too tired for love?"

"For sure."

"Sucks."

"I'm an independent young woman, Clint. And, like . . . I'm not just going to roll over and play some slut, you know."

"Wait, I thought love is, like, the greatest thing on Earth—"

"Duh. But sometimes you're tired."

I wish I could tell Zoë I don't know what "tired" feels like. Meanwhile, her molecules have shrunken to black and yellow spots—relaxing. She eventually falls asleep. I just lie there . . . trying not to babble to, you know, wake her up.

Then she sits up and, without saying anything, removes her T-shirt. I can't see her breasts, though, 'cause they're covered by this . . . "Bra," I say.

Zoë ignores me and falls back to sleep.

[resume log: 46.34]

In bed with Zoë, Father. Will resume mission. Soon. As my earthling friend Kips says, "No worries, motherfucker." Meanwhile, Zoë turned off lights to, like, invite the darkness in, I guess. Don't like the dark. The suit, meanwhile, per its temperature programming, has begun to "sweat." Like, too much—malfunctioning and shit. Legs and arm portions all wet. Question: If I don't sleep like earthlings, do I have to pretend to?

Thought: Will start mission. Like, in a minute.

Question: What's an earthly minute feel like?

[pause]

Zoë opens her eyes. Is all, "Gosh, you're sweaty—maybe you should take off your jeans when you sleep."

"Okay," I say, peeling off the jeans.

Little hairs stick out the skin. Strange. Zoë's staring at me all funny and saying, "You don't wear underwear?"

"I don't know, like . . . sort of."

"I guess that's hot."

"Thanks."

She runs her hand along the skin portion of the arm, and then says, "Oh my God!"

"What's wrong?"

"You have, like . . ."

"What?"

"Nothing."

"What?"

"You have, like . . . nothing."

"What?"

"A really big dick—oh God, I can't believe I said it."

I'm all, looking down at what she's looking at, which, according to the colloquilator, is a "penis." Stupid colloquilator. "Wait," I say, "you call that a 'dick'?"

"You mean—you think it's small?"

I don't know what to say, so I'm all silent and shit. Then Zoë says, "It's fucking huge."

"I guess."

"Gosh, you're so insecure, Clint."

"I am?"

"Yes."

"Fuck."

"It's okay, all guys are," she says, then touches the top portion of the dick. It grows even bigger. "Oh my God," Zoë says. She gets off the bed, and then stands there looking at me, turning all gray inside. Before I get a chance to, like, make her less afraid of my dick, she hurries out of the room.

I follow her into the bathroom. Meanwhile, this gray web-like thing has formed inside her as she sits on the toilet. I turn the light switch on. Kip is lying in the tub portion.

"Ahh!" Zoë screams. "Goddamnit, Kip! Why didn't you tell me you were in here?"

"Needle!" I say, noticing the thing on the floor near the tub.

"Duh," Zoë says, talking low like. Meanwhile, Zoë's got grass behind her eyes. "I'm sorry," I say, "that you're sad."

When I go to hug her she looks up at me but I guess my penis, like, takes up all her vision, 'cause she's saying, "You're starting to, like, totally freak me out."

"I can't control this thing, Zoë."

"Clint, just . . . oh my God it's, like—an arm!"

"Whoa," Kip says from the tub, "you can solve world peace with that thing, brother."

✳   ✳   ✳

I follow her into the bedroom. She sits on the bed, staring at me. Then she reaches out and touches the dick, and for a moment my molecules begin to rattle. But she is all, "I know you're horny, but it's just . . . like I told you, I'm tired, and, I don't know, I barely know you."

I lay down next to her on the bed, and she all turns over, inside these orange bubbles erupting out from her little silver pond.

I don't want to lie here pretending to sleep.

I will start the mission. Now.

[resume log: 45.90]

Father, penis portion of suit is too big. Question: Can scientists fly a smaller version in a separate craft?

According to mission instructional, I was supposed to receive messages from you, Father. Have received nothing. Question: Why're you, like, ignoring me—are you busy with the committee?

[44.87]

Climbed "stairs" to roof portion of house and am sitting on a "chaise" thing, staring at the stars in this galaxy.

Meanwhile, light ignites inside the building across road. Inside room I see a bed, and what appears to be a male earthling, standing there all naked; his penis appearing much smaller than mine—lucky him!

Naked female walks in. Uh-oh.

"Breasts." She has breasts, Father! They grab each other. Male now kisses female's breasts while she looks up at the ceiling, inside her green flowers growing.

Suddenly, female falls to floor—stands on her knees portion. Begins to eat male's penis. Male smiles. Female stands. Penis, like, still there. Thought: Maybe she didn't eat it.

Male and female now lie on bed. Inside their bodies a light blinks . . . and then the blinking turns to this yellow joined fist like thing. Thought: Should climb up the side of the house to get closer look. Question: If they see me looking into the window, will they get scared or invite me inside the room?

Follow-up thought: Feeling suddenly very alone.

Beyond the building, something erupts in the ocean. It looks like a . . . "Fire," I say. Question: Does fire grow on water? Thought: Prefer to, like, watch the naked earthlings.

Female sitting on male's head—inside her body all these red wires are twisting, tangling through themselves.

[44.44]

Have begun mission.

Darkness has invaded roads. Cars parked outside the earthling homes. Thought: Los Angeles sector of California made up of earthlings whose homes are one, like, constructions guarded by all kinds of vegetation and stuff; or two, made of blankets and tents earthlings like Kip use to sleep on the beach.

Father, I'm not going to bother telling you about the mission anymore, 'cause you don't seem to care. You know what, fuck it, Father. I am no longer recording for you. It is the committee I record for, 'cause that's what I promised I would do per the mission.

Meanwhile, gigantic car whose doors are all open. Inside it, a black, male earthling is removing "socks" from his feet. When he sees me, he smiles.

Am all, "Hello."

He's all, "How you doin'?"

Am all, "Okay. What's your name?"

He's all, "Carl."

[pause]

What if Zoë comes back with me to my planet? This way, we can, like, take our time and maybe make some earthling love in the craft on the way back.

Best thought I've had on Earth!

When I return to the house, she's wearing these yellow things on her hands, and I'm looking at them before I think, gloves! Then I'm thinking it's all cool that I remembered not to say it out loud when Zoë's all, "Where'd you go last night—why didn't you call? You can't treat me like some slut, you know. I don't even know your cell phone number!"

"But—"

"You know, Clint, I don't care about your fucking money. Remember that. You can't just treat me like some . . . second-class citizen and stuff."

"But Zoë, I just—"

"You on something?"

I tell her I met Carl, that we gave away all this money; she's all one, not really listening or two, not believing me. I think it's two. "Anyway," she's saying, talking real fast, "this house is a *disaster*. I'll need some money to buy some cleaning supplies. The dirt, like, totally reminds me of my mom's house. I hate that. I hate messy houses. Life's, like, way too short. Oh, and I'm thinking we should replace this assed-out couch. Besides, I think Kip puked on it. Yeah. He's going places."

Inside she is filled with anxiety, these little pointy things appearing around her veins. Then she's saying again I was wrong for leaving her alone last night, and I'm all, "You were mad 'cause of my big dick."

"You don't get it, do you?"

"Get what?"

"Like, we're trying to build a relationship here, I mean, or so I thought—and you just treat it like . . . I'll have you know I'm *not* one of your paid servants that you grew up with, Clinton."

According to the colloquilator, a "servant" is *one who serves another*. Suddenly I'm all thinking I thought of the perfect, like, response. In fact, I'm spinning inside the suit I'm so happy at the thought of it. "I'm *your* servant, Zoë."

"Whatever!"

All of a sudden I begin to shrink inside the suit—confused—and find myself saying, "Females are, like . . . *crazy*."

"How *dare* you reduce me to a *female*?"

"Zoë," I say, walking toward her, but then I don't know what to say, and besides, she's all walking over to the sink and burying her hand inside this white, bubbling puddle of water. "We need supplies, Clint!"

"You can take all my money, Zoë, I don't care."

"You should go to a doctor."

"What the fuck is that supposed to mean?"

"Don't swear at me like that."

"Sorry."

"Did you eat, Clint?"

"Yes," I lie, "with Carl."

"Look, I'm sorry, to, like, nag you. . . . But I'm worried about you. You don't sleep. You have, like, no body fat on you—and you talk out the side of your mouth, which is, like . . . looks like you're on coke all the time."

And I can't run, I feel like saying. Either it's Zoë or earthling or just the Earth, but whatever it is, I'm fucking confused. I have a mission! I want to tell her. But I can't babble the truth. Sucks.

"Are you okay, Clint?"

"Yeah," I lie.

Zoë's all smiling now as she stares at me, "Hey. I have an idea—you want to help me clean?"

She looks all pretty, meanwhile, standing there with her peanut butter hair and zits on her face. I want to press my lips to hers, but, like, for some reason I think she'll get mad.

*　*　*

Am meant to "wipe down grime on the surfaces" with this stuff called Lysol that looks like something found on a neighboring planet. I'm sitting on the bathroom floor, thinking of Carl, this black earthling I met on a road in the darkness earlier. Carl wore a red blanket around him and pushed a vehicle called a "shopping cart," which we filled with money I got from, like, thirty banks; and then gave the money to homefree earthlings on the beach. Each earthling filled with blue or red tongues inside whenever they saw the money. "I like giving," I told Carl at a place called a "diner." "Giving is God," Carl said, "I know this much." His teeth were the color of the urine Kip left in the toilet before Zoë yelled at him to "flush!"

Carl ordered the steak and eggs, saying, "I want to feel like a millionaire for a moment." Compared to all earthlings I've seen, Carl has these green and blue clusters inside his head that are, like, constantly blinking. I was thinking his brain was, like, too powerful when Carl shoved all this steak in his mouth and said, "Know something—I think you're a damn angel." According to colloquilator, an "angel" is *one who is employed by God.* "Yeah," I told Carl, "whatever the fuck that means."

"What a mouth you have on you, boy!"

I asked Carl why there were so few, like, black earthlings on Venice Beach. He started explaining the difference between the black and the white earthlings, the slavery, the pain, "the ridicule," the "genocide in Africa," the "nigger word" and all this stuff that almost sounds, like, made up. I'm all, "That just sounds fucking awful, Carl." His whole body shook when he laughed. He was all, "That's one way of looking at it. Son, let me tell you, I tend to look at it with what I call an eye of peace." "Eye of Peace?" "That's right." "What the fuck is that supposed to mean?" Egg slipped out his mouth when he laughed. "Wait, Carl, like, why is there so much death on Earth, and, you know, disease and war and all that?" He said it's up to the creator above to decide that. I looked out the window at the pink stars and said, "Is the creator, like, from another planet?"

"Maybe so," Carl laughed, his big body rattling. You know, I was all thinking how much I liked Carl when he got all serious and said, "They sent you—didn't they?"

"Wait—who do you mean *they*?"

"You know goddamn well who I mean."

Fuck! Maybe Carl was sent by the committee.

Carl drank water, staring at me and said, "Son, I hear voices. Don't act like you don't *know*."

"Voices?"

"Don't sit there like you don't fucking *know*."

"What kind of voices, Carl?"

"Mostly they come from the goddamn radio. Matter of fact, other day . . ." Carl leaned across the table so that his shirt was all hanging over his food and said, "They told me that they's a dog on the beach who wants me dead. Now what kind of dog wants a man dead?"

"A *douchey* dog?" I said, 'cause I didn't know what to say. In fact, suddenly nothing on Earth made sense. A dog wanting to kill an earthling?

Meanwhile, Carl wiped his mouth with a white napkin, then poured coffee into his mouth. "By the way," Carl said, and then chewed some more, "you look *damn* familiar. You an actor?"

"No."

"Why don't you eat, son?" Carl leaned over again. "It's not like you can't *afford* it."

I smiled at Carl, but inside my molecules were all bumping against one another as I decided that Carl had a disease, one that had something to do with the power of electricity in his head. Strange. So I was all, "Carl! We have a house. You should sleep there."

Pink particles, meanwhile, were expanding throughout the sky that'd all turned the color of the sidewalk as Carl and I returned to the house. When he saw it, though, the green and blue clusters in his head started to blink all fast like and then his body filled with gray liquid and he said, "I know who's in there."

"Who, Carl?"

"You a dumb fool, you know that? You act like you an angel, but I know what you up to." He started pushing his shopping cart away, and I was all, "Carl, it's okay—just come inside and shit." And then he started to run, and so I started to run. But I can't run! So I walked as fast as I could after Carl but it was no use—he disappeared around the corner.

Zoë comes in the bathroom and is all, "What're you doing?" You know, we don't have "surfaces" where I'm from. But I can't tell her that.

She's all, grabbing the towel from the hand portion of my suit, "Oh, just let me do it!"

Meanwhile, I'm watching her, her face wet with sweat, her insides swelling with these blue bubbles of water.

"You are pretty, Zoë."

"Thanks." Her face melts with this smile. I find myself smiling, a sensation I like, 'cause it makes my molecules tingle. So I'm watching the leg portions under her jeans that have been ripped into shorts, and without any warning the penis starts to grow again.

"Fuck!" I say.

"What's wrong?"

I'm all walking out of the room so she won't see it, "Nothing."

"Look, Clint," she's saying from the kitchen, "it's just hard to live with someone who can't even do a simple household chore, you know? Plus . . . I'm getting my period."

According to the colloquilator, a "period" is *the character used to mark the end of a sentence.* Yeah, whatever the fuck that means. Thankfully, the penis shrinks, and I enter the room all smiling douchely at her, pretending I totally get what she's saying.

"I appreciate you, like, understanding me."

"Thanks, Zoë."

"You know, I was thinking, like, you renting the house and all and us sleeping in the same bed . . . maybe we should go out for dinner or something, like—a date. How's that sound?"

According to the colloquilator, a "date" is *an engagement for an entertainer to perform.* "What the fuck is a date, Zoë?"

"Can't you just *stop*, like, philosophizing for once?"

"Sorry," I say, thinking I'll have to pretend to eat and stuff, but that's okay. 'Cause maybe if I make her happy, she'll let me, you know, make love.

[resume log: 45.76]

Totally time to start mission. But, first . . .

On "date" at a restaurant called Lily's in the Venice sector. Earthlings in restaurant appear to have extremely clean clothing, their bodies all filled with red and white balls, many of them smiling as they insert food into mouths.

Thought: Eating makes earthlings happy—homefree earthlings don't have money to buy food.

Meanwhile, food appearing on plates being carried out by earthlings whose bodies are filling with black, anxiety pointy things.

Earthling wearing strange outfit asks where we'd like to sit, and I'm all, "Waiter," as we're following him.

"Yes?" another one dressed in the same outfit says to me.

Thought: Have got to stop saying stuff out loud!

When we sit down, Zoë looks at this gigantic piece of paper and is all, "Uh-oh."

"What's wrong and shit?"

"It's so much more expensive than I thought. Gosh, you have to be, like, rich to eat here."

"I have money, Zoë."

"Clint, I can't keep taking your money."

"It's not mine."

"Whose is it?"

"The bank's."

"Very funny."

Green squares form inside, only to dissolve to blue bubbles. Happy. She reaches across the table, touching my hand; inside the suit I am beginning to expand so much that suddenly she says, "Ouch."

"What?"

"No, it's just—I got one of those shocks from your hand."

Oops. Meanwhile, the "waiter" is standing over us. "Have you decided?"

"I'll have the steak frits?" Zoë says.

"Freets," says the waiter in what sounds like a different language.

"Oh," Zoë says and smiles at me, "it's all going to end in the same place."

"The toilet?" I say, suddenly happy that I figured something out.

Zoë starts laughing, her shoulders rattling. Black pointy things inside waiter turn to red cubes as he walks away.

"Huh," Zoë says, "I think we pissed him off."

"Oops."

"Totally. We shouldn't be, like, immature, you know?"

"Totally," I say, not knowing what else to say. Thought: I like this "date." Much better than stupid mission. Follow-up thought: Should defect and go on dates all the time with Zoë.

[pause]

Shouldn't have thought that!

"So," Zoë's saying, "what do you want to eat?"

"What?"

"Aren't you hungry?"

"Uh," I say, thinking my suit's all going to smell when I put food into it, "nah."

Orange cubes form inside Zoë's head. Confusion. But then this little light begins to blink. Anger. "I'm worried about you, Clinton."

Am all, trying not to sound *philosophical*, "Worrying is stupid."

"Let's face it, Clint." She all leans across the table and talks low like, "You have a drug problem."

"Like Kip?"

"Are you trying to stay thin to, like, be an actor? Or don't tell me your parents put all this pressure on you to go on auditions and stuff. Wait, are you, like, Clint Eastwood's grandkid or something?"

"No."

The waiter stands next to me like he wants to join our "date."

"Sorry about that, sir," he's saying. "So. Have you decided?"

I look down at the menu and then say out loud, *"Entrecote Grillée Sauce Béarnaise Ou Au Poivre."*

"Ah!" says the waiter, smiling. *"Vous avez un accent Parisien. Vous avez grandi a Paris?"*

"Qu'est-ce que le diable est Paris?"

"Ouais, je vois ce que vous voulez dire. Paris est une pute. De toute facon . . . le saumon. Bon choix, mon gars."

As the waiter walks away, this green tongue erupts inside of Zoë, and she's all smiling at me. "Clinton, that was, like, *way* hot."

"Hot?"

"Your speaking French."

"Me speaking what?"

She consumes water and says, "Gosh, you are so modest."

I smile back at her, not sure what's going on. I seem to have just, like, spoken in a strange language.

"So where'd you learn French?"

"Uh . . . instructionals and stuff."

"Did you go to school in France?"

I have to change the subject before Zoë keeps asking questions I can't answer. I'm all, "Zoë, let's make love."

"Here?"

"Yes!"

She looks around the room, then says in a lower voice, "Say it in French and I'll consider it."

I think about this for a while and then am all, "Fuck!"

Thought: Can only speak in other language when other earthling says something in that language. Can't seem to do it on my own. Will never make love now.

Zoë's all stuffing bread into mouth. Then, when she finishes eating the bread, she's all, "Can I be frank?"

Frank is an earthling name. Strange. "I guess," I say, "but I prefer you to be Zoë."

She laughs so hard water comes out of her mouth. "Silly. Anyway, I have to be honest. I realized, you know, you don't like to talk about your past. But it's only our first date . . . although we totally live together. Anyway, I just want to say that, like, I respect that. Like, when you're ready, I'm open to hear—okay?"

"Totally!"

I grab Zoë's hand across the table, and inside her this thin plant thing begins to grow. "I'm so glad I met you, Clinton."

"I'm glad I met me too," I say, trying to make her laugh, and she does!

Zoë's all talking about her douchebeat dad, who sent her a letter from jail saying he wants "custody" of her; but she wants nothing to do with him. 'Cause, she's saying, if he listened to her once in a while he'd understand that she doesn't respect him enough to want to live with him. An orange wall is rising up inside her now when the waiter starts placing plates of food on our table.

"I've never liked salmon," Zoë says, looking at my plate, on which this orange block lies. I try and think of this fish swimming into the ocean, but I can't imagine it. Then I'm all, wondering what it's going to smell like later on, "Maybe I shouldn't eat it then?"

"Clinton. Please! Eat. It's good for you. Don't make me worry about you."

I watch the other earthlings using "forks" to place food in their mouths. So I pick up the fork, use it as, like, a device to put little bits of salmon in mouth portion of suit. Meanwhile, Zoë's watching me as she uses a knife to open her steak.

"Chew, Clint!"

I begin to "chew," only I think I'm doing it too fast 'cause Zoë's all, "Slowly."

"Slowly. Right."

"Clinton, don't talk with your mouth full." Now she's staring at me. "Know something . . . I realize you don't want to talk about your family. And that's totally cool—but I can tell you were totally ignored."

"Totally!"

"What about your mother?"

"She evap—"

Zoë eats a portion of the steak and then is all, "She what?"

"I don't remember her."

"She died?"

"Yes."

"Aw, Clint, I'm so sorry." Suddenly, this pink liquid runs down

Zoë's throat inside, spilling down into that silver pond of hers.

"How old were you?"

"I don't remember."

"Just a baby? That's even sadder."

"Totally."

"You ever, like, have dreams of her?"

According to the colloquilator, "dreams" *are comprised of images, ideas, emotions, and sensations that occur involuntarily during sleep.* Great. I don't fucking sleep.

Am trying to think of Mother now; imagining what she looked like. Can't. Only seeing a bunch of pink molecules, taking shape of a circle.

"I dream . . . that she is a circle," I tell Zoë.

"Huh."

"Totally."

"And?"

"And what?"

"Like, that's it?"

"Uh . . . she is a circle, and then she, like, turns into a square."

"Wow, that's really abstract, Clint. What do you think it means?"

"Means?"

"Duh. All dreams mean something."

"That she, like, is made up of molecules!"

"Hmm—wow, that's kind of deep. Gosh, dreams are so weird, right?"

"Totally!"

Meanwhile, the food is disintegrating in my suit—I know it, 'cause I can feel it vibrating as it, like, breaks it down.

"What's that smell?" Zoë says.

"Must be the kitchen."

"Smells like burning rubber or something."

So I stop eating, and Zoë's all, "Clint, you have to eat."

Darkness has invaded the Venice sector. We're walking along the sidewalk, most of the earthlings passing filled with blue liquid in their stomach portions.

"You have such beautiful skin, Clint," Zoë says, grabbing my hand. I have to try and make sure not to shock her, so I shift to the right side of the suit, which, like, makes me walk all weird.

"I'm so jealous," she says. "You have, like, no zits."

"I like your zits."

We're all walking with our hands touching, when suddenly Zoë screams, and I'm thinking I killed her with my electric current or something. "Oh my God," she says, "have you ever tried Pinkberry?"

Zoë is shoving this spoon filled with a strange, white substance into my mouth. Am hoping it won't smell. Meanwhile, earthlings dressed in clean clothing also are shoving white substance into their mouths, their insides filled with silver blocks for some reason.

"Thanks for dinner," Zoë says, this green plant like thing growing inside her again.

"Whatever."

"Say you're welcome, Clinton."

"You're welcome, Clinton."

Zoë rattles with laughter. So I say it again, and she keeps laughing. "I love the way you talk," she says, "it's adorable."

I lean forward and press lips to her lips, and I'm all, breaking apart inside when she says, "Ouch!"

"What?"

"I got shocked again. Why does that keep happening?"

"Fuck!"

"No . . . it's probably my fault. I probably walked on the carpet too much with my socks when I was cleaning earlier. Been feeling that a lot lately. Or who knows—maybe we're electric."

Meanwhile, I contract into the stomach portion of the suit, managing to move lips toward hers. Feeling her tongue enter this time, only difficult to feel as I've shrunken to the size of a fork.

Then I'm all looking at Zoë's zits and her smile and suddenly I expand and rattle at the same time.

I am happy. I am loving my time on Earth!

"This was a fun date, Clinton."

"Totally!"

Zoë licks the spoon and says, "For sure."

"Can we make love now?"

Inside this plant thing melts into this orange pond. "Uh . . . don't you remember, Clint?"

"Remember what?"

"That I'm getting my period."

"Oh, yeah."

"And you still want to, like, make love?"

"Can we?"

[resume log: 44.98]

Sunlight has returned, spilling through the windows and shit. Zoë all mad at me 'cause I said I want to make love to her while she's "on her period." On the way home, she said, "Ew! It just grosses me out that you want to do it—wait, are you're, like, one of those spoiled rich kids who always gets what they want?"

We walked home in silence, all the cars roaring past us and shit as I began to suddenly think that Earth is a confusing planet and its females just make it, like, impossible to understand.

[44.70]

Looking out window. Zoë asleep. Little black animal with white line on it walks up to palm tree. Question: Am I too much of an idiot for this Earth?

[44.20]

Fuck it.

Am beginning the mission. No more confusion. Time to face the douche.

[pause]
I'm afraid of this stupid mission but also afraid if I don't start I'll just end up a total loser. I know I can do it, I just know it. What? Something's happening. Am getting a message!

[IN RESPONSE TO YOUR QUERY . . .
ACCORDING TO AN ANALYSIS, WE HAVE DETERMINED
THAT THE PENIS PORTION OF YOUR SUIT IS
INDEED LARGER THAN THE AVERAGE EARTHLING
MALE'S. HOWEVER, WE HAVE DETERMINED THAT
ITS PRESENCE, NO MATTER HOW PROMINENT,
IS NOT SIGNIFICANT ENOUGH TO HINDER
THE MISSION. IN CONCLUSION: WE WILL NOT
BE SENDING AN ALTERNATIVE PENIS IN A
SEPARATE CRAFT. CONTINUE MISSION AS
PLANNED.]

[resume log: 44.01]
Fuck!

[pause]
I'm not going to respond to that stupid message. But if I were, I'd maybe ask why a certain Father can't respond to me personally. And why aren't they answering all my questions?

✳ ✳ ✳

I look out the window to see the sun, like, gone, the sky all filled with clouds. Everything gray. Meanwhile, Kip's sleeping on the couch. Zoë's eating something out of a bowl in the kitchen. Earthlings—they never stop eating! How long could I, like, last in this suit if I have to keep pretending to do stupid earthling stuff. Eating. Sleeping. Or defecating—ah, if only I could defecate! Everything would be *so* much easier.

But I have to be truthful: It's the mission I'm, like, worried about. Can't keep avoiding it. Am standing in the kitchen near Zoë when I find myself saying, "Zoë."

"Yes?"

"There's something I have to do."

She's all, chewing, "What?"

"I have to go somewhere. A house."

"Whose?"

"Someone my father knows. Can you ascertain a car?"

"Ascertain a car? What're you, on crack? I don't have a license. Wait—I think Kip, like, bought one with all the money you gave away. Kip!"

Kip does not wake up.

"Kip, wake up!" Zoë says, and then presses a toe onto his chest. "Clint needs a ride somewhere."

Zoë then grabs a bag and wraps her arms around me. Then presses herself so hard against me; I'm all hiding in the back of the suit so that I don't shock her. "So," she says, "I have to hang with my mom for a couple of nights. How about, when we get back, we go on, you know, another date?" She puts her lips to my ear and is all, "And maybe we can . . . you know?"

"Make love?"

"Shh!" Zoë says. Then she kisses me on the cheek, and runs upstairs.

"Kip," I say, "I need a ride."

"Do I look like a bitch?" Kip says on the couch, eyes still closed.

"What?"

"Do I look like a *bitch*?" Kip says, eyes still closed.

"I don't know, like . . . sort of."

"You're supposed to say no."

"I don't know what a bitch is, Kip."

"You philosophical mother—it's from a movie, man. Just say I don't look like a bitch."

"No, Kip, you do not look like a bitch."

"Then why you tryin' to fuck me, Clint?" Kip's all rattling with laughter when Zoë walks downstairs and says, "So—what's the word, yo?"

We're flying at light-speed in Kip's car that he bought with money I gave him. It's blue and it rattles so much when it drives I have to, like, stay in the top portion of the suit, near the head, or else my molecules will start to shake.

"Thanks to you, brother," Kip's saying, the wind, like, blowing through the car, "I picked this badboy up. You like her?"

"It's a her?" I say.

"It's totally bad for the environment," Zoë says, sitting in the front seat.

"What the fuck's the environment ever done for me?" Kip says.

"You're a dick," Zoë says.

"Chill out, babe, I'm just kidding."

"Uh, I'm not your babe, Kip, thank you very much."

"Women," Kip's saying, looking at the mirror so that he can see me in the back. "Know what I'm saying, brother?"

Meanwhile, I'm watching all the cars driving past us—there must be, like, thousands, each one of them coughing out this toxic substance that rises into the air.

A black aircraft, like, hovers over the cars, looking down on them. Helicopter! I think, glad I didn't say it out loud.

Earthlings, including Kip, are driving so fast no wonder there's so much death on Earth; they just love to go fast.

"Where we dropping you again, brother?"

I look down at my fingernail monitor and say, "Mulholland Drive."

"Gotcha."

"Is your father going to be there?" Zoë says, turning around so that I can see her pretty face. Meanwhile, inside her head she's turned yellow, with black dots growing—she seems worried.

"No," I say.

"You're not, like, going to buy drugs or something, are you?"

"Mind your business, man," Kip says, "a man's got to *breathe*."

"No," I tell Zoë, "it's a friend of my father's."

"Oh. Okay," she says, staring out the window, "I trust you."

We are stopped in what Kip calls "hella traffic" when he starts explaining that he has an addiction to the substance known as "heroin." Zoë and I remain all silent while he speaks, 'cause he's all, "I'm saying this because I trust you kids." "Kids?" Zoë says. "Like, why do you talk like you're forty?" But Kip ignores this and starts talking about "How it all started with a band named the Deathly Grateful." And how he saw them play when he was ten years old, where he took his first "acid trip" and then had to go to the hospital; and I'm thinking this band doesn't sound all that grateful, when Kip's saying he eventually moved to California 'cause "Karma told me so, brother." But when he took a job at a restaurant, he ended up impregnating the boss's daughter. He said "money and me never liked each other—matter of fact, we had an agreement to stay away from one another, know what I'm saying, brother?" Eventually, he ended up sleeping in a tent on Venice Beach.

Before he used drugs, Kip had, like, dreams the size of planets, he's saying. Dreams to act in films. Dreams to play in bands. "I'll tell you something, man. I never dreamed of sleeping on the motherfucking beach."

Kip explains that this rich, vast land whose states are united does not pay much attention to its homefree earthlings; it doesn't

give "health care for starters, man." I'm staring at toxic smoke rising out of a gigantic car when I tell Kip that I'm all sorry for his
past. And he's all, "Let me tell you something, brother, even if I
grew up with a rich daddy like yours, I'd still be in this mess. Matter of fact, I'd probably be more fucked. Let me teach you something you'll never forget, okay?" "Okay, Kip." "Slow down!" Zoë
says. "You ready?" "I'm ready, Kip." "Stop tailgating," Zoë says.
"You and everyone on this motherfucking planet," Kip says, "is
responsible for ourselves." I think about this and then say, "That
makes sense, Kip."

Meanwhile, thousands of earthlings are trapped in their cars,
smoke getting all coughed out their engines. I'm thinking I can't
talk of my past; can't tell Zoë and Kip I'm all worried one, the
douche will sense me and have me evaporated before I even get
close to him and two, Father will probably get into serious trouble
with the central committee.

"You can go to rehab," Zoë says.

"Oh, I'm going to," Kip says, "next week—right after the Burning Man festival."

I want to ask what a man burning has to do with anything, but
I don't want to sound dumb. In fact, I'm starting to wish I didn't
have this douchey mission, and I could just spend time with my
friend Kip and "my girl" Zoë. As I'm thinking this, something has
gone wrong with the suit. That is, I can't move suddenly. I contract
into the head portion so that I can have more strength to shift it.
Nothing. Fuck!

"Famous last words," Zoë's saying to Kip.

"Listen, bee-yotch, I don't—"

"Don't call me a bee-yotch, you loser."

"Don't call me a loser, you bee-yotch."

Zoë touches her hair, staring out the window. Meanwhile, I can't move—and am worried if they look back I'll look dead. "Look," Zoë says, looking out the window still, "I'm sorry for calling you a loser, Kip. Clint's right—it's a stupid word no one should use."

"I'm sorry too," Kip says. Then he lights a cigarette on fire, and blows smoke out the window and says, "Women, brother . . . they're nuts—but I worship them."

"Whatever, Kip," Zoë says.

"Look, kids. Do me a favor, all right?"

"We're not kids, Kip."

"Whatever you do, don't grow up to be me, okay?"

"Okay, Kip," I say, but my mouth didn't move when I said that. Hopefully, they didn't notice. I travel up and down the suit, from the legs to the arms, as fast as I can.

We're stopped near a "wooded section" when I'm all, "Is this Mulholland Drive?"

"Sure is, brother."

"Stop!"

"Yes, sir."

"But there are, like, no houses around," Zoë says.

"I don't want you to see the house," I find myself saying. Wait, my mouth moved! I move an arm. Another arm. Good.

"Aw, Clint. You're embarrassed of your wealth, aren't you? This friend of your father is rich, huh?"

"Uh, yes?"

"This rich sonofabitch got a pool, brother?"

"I don't know, Kip."

"A hot tub?"

"Kip, we're not invited. Don't be rude."

"I'm just sayin', man, if this rich dude's got some chlorinated water in the backyard, we're the poolest people in L.A. County right now. Ain't that right, Clint?"

"Uh," I say, not knowing what to say, "yes?"

"Wait," Zoë says, "how do you know it's not, like, a woman who owns the house?"

"Hey, you want to borrow my lighter?"

"No. Why?"

"To burn your training bra."

"Bite me, Kip!"

"You wish."

"Oh, and FYI: I don't wear a training bra anymore."

The car, meanwhile, rattles to a stop, and Kip gets out and opens its gigantic door. I step out, and then walk around to the other side so that I'm closer to the wooded section.

"Lates," Kip says.

"Bye, Clinton." Zoë pulls her body outside the car and closes her eyes and presses her lips into the air so that I'm, like, lowering my lips and then we're kissing when the car roars and drives away.

"Don't forget our date!" Zoë shouts before the car disappears around the corner.

"Bye," I say, suddenly looking at a tree, envying that it just gets to stand there and not have to deal with any stupid mission.

[resume log: 43.38]

Something went wrong with the suit in Kip's car. Couldn't move for a while. Question: Is it something I did?

Area where douche lives sits so high up that, like, through the trees, I can see what looks like an entire planet of lights whose crazy flickering reminds me of Zoë for some reason. Aircrafts hovering in purple air over Los Angles sector. Lots of palm trees down there. Strips of black pavement. Gigantic buildings in the distance. Star vibrating in the sky . . . fumes getting coughed out from cars.

Per instructional, using hands portion of suit to dig into the Earth.

[42.91]

Suit buried under soil. Slipping out ear cavity of suit, through the dirt—retrieving the apprehension device from the sphincter of the suit. Apprehension device is a small, orange ball that's *capable of neutralizing defector for capture.*

So freeing to be out of the suit!

Douche's house, from the road, appears to be wall made of "translucent" glass.

I float over the wall.

House made of two gigantic glass boxes sitting next to each other; palm trees taller than any I've seen. Sensing he's in his earthling suit, standing behind the house. Worried he might sense me.

Must not worry; must not fear.

Drifting through open window of the house now . . . seeing a female earthling looking into the refrigerator; her hair looking like it's been rubbed with carrots. Cluster of sticks inside her stomach. She's longing—possibly for a baby earthling. Which he can't give. Douche.

She closes refrigerator and begins using a knife to slice into a piece of what looks like red fruit. Drifting into the gigantic room that's got some black furniture sitting on top of a white rug. Drifting toward back, feeling all bad that she's married to a being who doesn't even, like, need to eat.

Thought: This is going to be easy. Sensing—he is definitely in the back of the house.

Drifting over the pool whose water is black for some reason; edge of pool surrounded by vegetation—some prickly shit; pink and blue flowers and stuff; palm trees trying to reach the sky.

Thought: Our being is protected by his own premises.

Engaging the apprehension device.

I see him. He stands, earthling suit back to me; facing the flat land of flickering lights down below. He is holding a long, thin thing that looks like a wire. Snake!

Snake? Water is coming out of the *snake's* mouth. Strange. Drifting closer. Sensing that his being inside his suit is brittle.

Quickly, he turns around, water spraying at me. He can't sense me, I'm too young. Am contracting now, ascending into the air above the spray of water.

The skin of the suit, like mine, is too perfect for this Earth. His hair is long, looking like it's been mixed with sand and soil. Question: How can earthlings possibly mistake him for one of their own? Eyes and teeth sparkle. Face has a friendly expression.

Drifting over the pool now, saying, in our language, "I have come for you."

The eyes on his suit close. Inside, though, he begins to expand, these white and red triangles of electronic activity. Water spills out the snake.

Am all: "I'm going to ascertain you, I have you in my sight."

He walks in circles now, scanning the area. "How many are you—why can't I see you?"

"The committee requests your presence. You are constructing a film about our planet."

His suit rattles with laughter. Inside, he's turning sand like. Fear. "You have no idea what you're talking about."

"You are constructing a movie about our planet. It's a threat to our beings."

"Ah—you are a just a young idiot. *That's* why I can't see you."

Am all, "Don't call me an idiot."

"Nice comeback," he says in earthling English.

"You don't know anything about me," I find myself saying, suddenly shrinking into the size of a cigarette. "And you're, like, totally coming with me."

"What's your name?"

"I don't have to tell you that."

"Your earthling name, I mean. Look . . . it's small of me to call you an idiot. I apologize for that, it's just—you don't have to be so serious. We can talk this out. Come on—what's your name?"

"What do you care?"

"What're you afraid of?"

"I'm not afraid. Wait—you think I'm afraid?"

"Please. It's not like I'm asking for your real name—just your earthling name."

Am all, lowering so that my molecules almost touch the water of the pool, "Clint."

"Eastwood?"

"How'd you know?"

"Fools."

"Who?"

"No one on Earth's going to take you seriously with that name. Don't you get it? Indirectly you're named after my success."

"What the fuck is that supposed to mean?"

He laughs, and then the water stops spilling out the snake. "Look, it's as simple as this. Years ago my suit was designed to look like a standard but somewhat handsome, male earthling. And now that I've become a famous actor, these idiots figure they should design you after some other successful actor. It's a stupid formula."

Am all, ascending now: "No it's not!"

"Ah, I'm starting to see you now. I can tell that you're confused by everything."

"Earthlings are hard to understand."

[pause]

Fuck! Why did I just say that? Have to stay . . .

Focused.

Am revolving around the pool, trying to concentrate and shit when the douche is all, "I understand them perfectly."

"Who?"

"Earthlings, dummy."

"Don't call me that."

"Sorry. Just trying to lighten you up a bit."

"Wait, how do you understand earthlings?"

"Like Marlon Brando," he says in earthling English, taking a seat on the grass, "I come at it from the outside. I have what every single actor on Earth dreams of." He looks back, like he can see me, but he can't—I don't think—and says, "Alien perspective."

I'm all, hovering over the pool now, "The committee says that you've been losing attention from earthlings."

He stands up, walking back and forth now, holding the arm portion of his suit to the valley of lights like all its earthlings are listening. "If you don't mind me asking, what pleasure do you find in fulfilling this mission?"

"I don't have to, like, fucking answer that."

"You going to swear now?"

"You going to be douchey now?"

"Heh heh. You're such a youth. That's why I can't sense you. Actually, I have to say, you crack me up a little."

"An earthling told me that."

"Clint, do yourself a favor, all right? Return and tell the committee you see the goodness I'm doing for all earthlings through my movies. Better yet, stay for a while. Kick back. Enjoy what this incredible planet has to offer."

"What about your wife?"

"What about her?" Inside I can see that he's contracted into the stomach area of his suit.

"You can't give her what she wants."

He laughs.

"She's longing for something you can't give her."

"Do you enjoy," the douche says, trying to, like, talk about something else, "life back on that boring planet?"

"I don't know," I say, suddenly thinking I don't.

"Then why return?"

"'Cause I don't belong."

"Please! Every *minute* earthlings are moving into territories that, according to some law, they're not meant to inhabit. For instance, Mexicans pour into this country every day—do you know why?"

According to the colloquilator, a "Mexican" is—

"A chance to *dream*," the douche says, "a better life. A wealthier existence."

"But what if these douchicans, like, get captured?"

The douche laughs so hard his suit is, like, vibrating. "You know, your vocabulary, along with your imagination, is profoundly limited. Captured? Please. It's a gamble, man. It's a *thrill*!"

Inside I can see that he's shrunken into a blue ball of, like, wires—lies. I'm all, "I sense you're lying." His suit stops shaking as he sits down on a rock that's the color of Zoë's hair. "Don't you know that when you land on Earth, it can take years for your senses to adjust—or did the scientists forget to tell you this?"

"Wait," I say, suddenly thinking of all the earthlings whose insides I've, like, looked into and shit. "Are you fucking serious?"

"Clint, come on—quit this silly mission. Stay on Earth. Trust me. You won't regret it."

I find myself drifting so that I'm hovering next to his ear. Now, in silence, the two of us watch the Los Angeles sector below darken as millions of lights begin to flicker. "I fell in love," the douche is saying, "with an earthling woman when I first arrived. She was amazing—you would have really liked her, Clint. But she died in an car accident. Tragic. Trust me, I was shattered. And I came pretty quickly to understand what they refer to as 'depression.' Did you know that some of the best art on Earth emerged from the era of the Black Plague? Of course, you don't. But remember this, Clint: Good things come from tragedy. Anyhow, that mental . . . *muck* in which I found myself slithering around helped me discover acting. And so I worked on countless films, traveled the world, met all kinds of prominent people, blah blah blah . . . and, you know, eventually fell in love with my beautiful wife. Karen."

"Wait," I find myself saying, "what's earthling love like?"

He sits there all silent before saying, "Oh, gosh—utterly unimaginable?"

"Really?"

"Mysterious. Fun. Complex. Torturous. Joyous. Beyond comprehension, my friend."

"That's kind of what the scientists said and shit. Like, beyond logic."

Suddenly, without thinking, I'm telling him how I found myself enjoying Zoë's company. And he's saying I should stay in order to experience love with her; that he teaches earthlings how to preserve and nurture earthling love through his films. I tell him I thought love holds no logical value, that it can't be taught. "That's nonsense," he says, "typical of the committee to send a being on a fool's errand."

"I'm not a fool!"

"It's an expression. Sorry, you're just so innocent. Look, Clint, trust me on this. For what it's worth, stay. You'll come to love earthlings in ways you can't even imagine. And the sex! I mean, do you realize, what with our electronic impulses—we can give orgasms that most women can't dream of."

According to the colloquilator, an "orgasm" is *in no way related to your mission.*

Fuck!

I'm all revolving around a palm tree, wondering if I should ask what an orgasm means, when he gets off the chair and starts walking along the pool. I begin hovering in slow circles around him, just in case he tries to, like, escape and I need to apprehend him. He seems relaxed now, though, at least, inside his being is dissolving into a green fountain.

"I'm going to level with you, okay, Clint?"

"Okay."

"I did at one time have plans to develop a film about our planet. But I couldn't get the writers to come up with something that pleased me. Earthlings known as 'writers,' by the way, are impossibly moody beings. Anyway, the studio's put the project into turnaround. So the committee, if you think about it, is, in some ways, misinformed. You know I can't imagine what you're going through, by the way. When I arrived on this planet, I had enough instructionals to last me two years, and not a single one of them was sufficient."

I'm all, "Really?"

"Let me ask you something: Have your instructionals properly prepared you for the chaos of life down here?"

"No way!"

"There you go."

For some reason I want to make the douche laugh, so I'm all, "But weren't you, like, afraid to defecate?"

He's all laughing. "Uh, I believe you meant to use the word 'defect to—'"

"I was just making a—"

"Joke?"

He smiles as I lower myself beside his ear again. "Yes," I say, "a joke."

"Well, let's just say that *defecating* has been the best thing I've ever done."

Wait, I'm suddenly liking the douche! The thing is, although I don't want to tell *him* this, I've never actually seen a single member of the committee. For all I know, they don't even exist. Father used to never respond when I ask about them. Maybe *they* are the douches.

"Clint," he's asking now, "why would you ever leave a place of such profound mystery—a place where, in a single moment you can find bliss and wonderment and . . . true love? Okay, answer this: If you apprehend me, you'll have to leave at once, no? You'll have to leave this Zoë without ever seeing her again. Am I right?"

"Yes."

"Have you had sex with her?"

"You mean—"

"Fucking. Banging. Screwing. Making love—whatever."

"No. She's got her comma."

"Her what?" He laughs all calmly and shit, and inside I can see that he has formed into a black bar. Which, to me, appears to be truth. He's all, "You mean period? Anyway, that's just a natural part of the earthling female reproductive cycle. It comes once a month, and usually lasts a week or so. It'll be over soon, and then you can make love to her."

"Actually," I say, liking that I can finally babble the truth to somebeing, "she's afraid to make love 'cause my dick's too big."

Inside the suit his being forms a red, elongated shape, like a big knife. I think it's envy, but that makes no sense. He stands up, and then begins walking back and forth, looking out at all the lights. "How do *you* know this?"

"Know what?"

"Your penis—that it's too big."

"She said it was. Oh—and the scientists sent me this douchey message saying that even though it's big, it's still okay. I think they're just trying to make up for their mistake. Like, it's a malfunction, right? I knew it!"

"It's curious they made yours that way."

"Totally."

"Can I see it?"

"No!"

"Look, I don't want to suck it, I just want to see it."

"What the fuck is that supposed to mean?"

He's standing on one foot now as his body begins to lean forward, so that he looks like some sort of earthling bird. "I was referring," he's saying, "to the method female earthlings administer upon male earthlings as a means of . . . pleasure." He switches feet now and is all, "You know, incidentally, I almost played a homosexual in a film—but the producers worried I was too recognizable. Load of bullshit. Too bad, I would have killed that role. And probably won the Oscar. Wait a second!"

"What?"

"Your suit resembles a younger version of Clint Eastwood?"

"Yeah."

"Are you sure?"

"Earthlings are always saying I look like him."

Standing on one leg, he, like, spins around slowly and then claps his hands. "Excellent." Meanwhile, I'm looking at all the lights down below, all those millions of homefull earthlings—wondering how many of the females are sucking the dicks of the males. Wait, is Zoë doing that right now to some doucheling male? I'm all trying not to imagine her doing this when I'm expanding, like, without warning—occupying his entire backyard; growing to the point where I'm worrying I might not stop and . . . uh-oh. Maybe this is what happens when we evaporate. "Help," I say in our language.

"Stop that!"

"I *can't*."

My molecules are stretching over his pool, and then, like, expanding over a portion of the wooded area behind his house . . . stretching over the lights when he's all, "I see you now!"

"I . . . can't . . . help it!"

"Just relax yourself, you're just nervous."

"I can't."

"Hurry, before my wife sees you!"

"I can't control it!"

"Yes you can. Just relax, Clint. You can do it. Just concentrate."

I contract, and then find myself hovering near him again—suddenly as small as an earthling head. "This is too much," I tell him, feeling like I'm about to disappear. "Being on Earth, it's just . . . it's too fucking hard."

He's all, taking shape of that knife inside again, "I really want to see that suit of yours."

"Why?"

"I'll teach you all you need to know about earthling love, Clint. Culture, cuisine, sex, business, fame—the whole thing. But first, you'll appear in a movie with me. I can produce it. My agent can represent you. I have a fantastic publicist. You'll win an Oscar. I'll make you famous, Clint. Is the suit good-looking—striking? Is it raw or elegant. I'd *really* like to know."

"I don't know . . ."

"Scratch that. It's not your job to know anything. I'll take care of everything. Go get it."

"Wait," I say, "don't, like, order me around and shit. I'm supposed to be apprehending *you*."

He's all laughing, taking a seat again on the grass and looking
up at me. "Hmm, I can't see you anymore."

"You saw me."

"For a few seconds, yes. You're very young."

I'm not sure if he's lying.

"Listen," he's saying, "I already told you I'm not doing that
movie about our planet, right?"

"I guess."

"Well, that pretty much renders your mission moot."

"It does?"

"Clint Eastwood, I have what earthlings call a confession."

"You do?"

"Stop answering everything I say with a question."

"Stop telling me what to do."

"Forget it."

"No—wait . . . what's your confession and shit?"

"You're too immature to handle it. Forget I brought it up."

"Stop telling me what I am."

"Okay . . . here it is. The committee originally sent me on a mission to become an actor."

"No fucking way!"

"That's right. The committee lied to you, Clint. They thought
that if I were an actor I could learn more about the contemporary

human existence than in any other form. See, actors are more wor-shipped than politicians."

"That's what the scientists told me."

"Yep. Now that the research is over, they want me to return. You know, between you and me, it's not fair. I obeyed the order. I worked very diligently to assimilate for them. I mean, my friends, colleagues, marriage, investments, and so on. And they expect me to just *vanish* from this planet?"

I can't, like, believe what I'm hearing. It's weird, though, 'cause it kind of makes sense. After all, they made my suit after an actor. "Like," I say, "you want me to be in the movie? Like, to be an actor? Like you?"

"Here comes my wife. Earthlings can see us in our pure form, you know."

"They can?"

"Quick—go get in the suit. Wait a couple of hours or so. Then come to our gate, and press 040324 on the keypad, okay? Hurry!"

"Honey?" his wife says, standing on the other side of the pool now. In the dying light her skin appears pink. Seeing her standing there looking as beautiful as a tree or some shit, I'm imagining Zoë and me having a house like this on top of the hill.

"Yes, dear," he says in this douchey voice—weird to hear the way he talks to her; it's both soft and heavy, like male and female at the same time.

I begin drifting quickly back over the house and the gate, doing what he says, totally wanting this life on Earth.

[resume log: 42.60]
In the wooded section again. Mission on, like, hold. Just taking some time to . . .

[pause]
I enter the ground where I buried the stupid suit. When my molecules penetrate the soil I'm hit with this question: What if everything I've been told is false? I haven't met a single member of the committee. Maybe, I'm thinking, this is why Father ignores me, 'cause he's all afraid to admit the truth: that the douche was sent to become an actor.

Suddenly it's as if everything I've ever known is, like, gone— nothing makes sense.

You know, some things just have to be done without any elec- tricity of thought. Like, the more time I spend on Earth the more I realize this is not a good way to be, always filled with electricity; which is all I am. It's time I act like I was a solid piece of . . .

Shit!

The suit feels weird for some reason.

Anyway, no more electric currents, no molecules that can expand into all kinds of stupid shapes. It's time I acted like I'm a rock, a tree, a piece of pavement—a fire hydrant. Am acting only for myself now. Fuck Father. Fuck the committee. Fuck the mission!

Don't know what's happening, but right now suddenly all life on Earth and on my planet and maybe in every motherfucking galaxy in between everything and every being is so clear to me. It's like I understand the entire existence of all living things.

I emerge from the ground, determined to resume an existence as a free being who does what he chooses. Amazing, this Earth! One moment you're scared, and the next you're smiling.

It's really dark now but I don't give a fuck.

I am not afraid. I'm returning to talk to the douche because I want to do it.

Hmm. Am wiping dirt from my suit as I make my way back to the douche's house when I notice that something has, like, totally gone wrong within the suit. One, it feels like maybe someone had replaced it with a heavier one at that. Two, I can't seem to walk without looking like one of the homefree earthlings on the beach whose blood is filled with alcohol.

Cresume log: 42.30]
Suit, like, collapsed. Am lying on pavement now. Darkness hanging over me.

Question: Was the committee listening just now when I paused the log? Uh-oh. Must focus. Using hands now to drag suit across the pavement when I hear this roaring. . . .

"Truck," I find myself saying as the thing screams over me.

Cpause]
Can move the leg portions now, a little. Takes long time to cross the street. Finally, reach the douche's house and realize I've forgotten the numbers to the keypad.

"I'm such an idiot!"

All of a sudden I begin, like, to blink inside the suit to the point where I'm starting to lose vision . . . and then . . . falling down.

Face touching pavement. Question: Does this happen to earthlings; one moment they're filled with strength and the next they're losing control?

Am thinking I should have given Zoë more money. This way, she could give some to her mother and father in jail and Kip and Carl. Should have given more money to the homefree; should have just given money to all earthlings who need it in this vast land whose states are all united and shit.

Manage to stand up again. If I weren't such an idiot, I could open it with some sort of electric frequency, like the way my nose hair extracts money from bank machines.

A black car drives by, its driver all staring at me. Using the hands portions, I pull the rest of the suit over the gate.

Finally, after all this effort to engage and manipulate the suit, I'm, like, sitting on the top of the gate, staring at some yellow flowers that have been placed in the douche's front yard near this big rock, and all of a sudden I'm falling over until I land on the other side of the gate.

"Driveway!" I say, lips all touching pavement.

The douche is rushing out of the front door, and then he's . . . *running* down the driveway. "Wait, how'd you figure out how to run?"

Then I hear, "Honey?"

The douche, meanwhile, responds in earthling English. "Oh, it's just that kid I was telling you about."

"Is he okay? He looks injured."

"He's fine," says the douche, coming closer, "he's actually a gymnast."

"You sure he's okay, hon?"

"You were supposed to wait a couple of hours," he says to me as I lie on the pavement. "Do you even know what an hour is?"

"No."

"Idiot."

"Douche!"

"Don't call me that, you little shit."

"Don't call me, like, either of those!"

"Okay, okay . . . let's just be calm. Let's be cool. Now. Tell me what you did wrong to the suit."

"I didn't *do* anything wrong. It just shut down for some reason."

"Hmm," he says, standing over me as he, like, moves his hair from the eyes portion of his suit. "Did you put something into it—some sort of chemical?"

"Chemicals? No."

"Hon," his wife says, "you sure you don't need any help?"

"Not at all, babe, I can handle it!"

"Her name is 'babe'?"

"Do you realize," he's saying, lifting me by the arms portion, "that you look like an earthling whose legs are completely broken?"

105

He drops me.

And I'm all lying on the stomach portion, noticing, for the first time, a little creature walking really fucking fast between the little bits in the pavement. "Ants!"

The wife must be back, 'cause the douche is laughing in that foreign, soft way of his as he walks away. "Turns out, kid's been drinking. Went to a party at some producer's house. They went at it all night—from the looks of it. You know the pressures young actors face today."

"I thought you said he was a gymnast?"

"Oh, I was just being facetious, honey. You know me better than that. Actually, all sarcasm aside, he's researching a role for a biopic about—" The douche walks up the driveway, looking back at me as he's saying, "Bart Conner."

"Poor thing," the wife says, "should I get him some aspirin?"

"No, no. Wait, can you do me a favor, though, babe? Check to see if I left the refrigerator door open in the basement?"

Meanwhile, I'm watching an ant running with what looks like a piece of food on its back. "Crumb!" I say, suddenly loving the colloquilator. Thought: At one point earthlings didn't have stores to buy food from—of this much I know from an instructional. Another thought: Can't seem to think, like, clearly for some reason.

A gigantic door opens in a way I've never seen a door open before—from bottom to top—and the douche appears wheeling a vehicle in front of him, similar to Carl's shopping cart, only it's red. "Okay," he says, his hair all bouncing as he pushes the vehicle. I'm all, face lying on the driveway, "How'd you figure out how to run?"

"Don't speak," he says, and then, in one quick motion he, like, lifts me and drops me into this wheeled vehicle, and I'm all of a sudden looking up at the stars vibrating as the douche wheels me up the driveway.

9

[resume log: 41.50]

Sitting in a chair made of metal. In room with low ceilings—a round window whose, like, other side appears to be water. Thought: Being held captive under ocean.

Question: Why am I wearing shiny black shoes, black pants, a strange, white shirt, and a douchey-shaped tie?

[pause]

"Tuxedo!" I say in earthling English, testing the colloquilator. Something else is different, though—I can move the arms and legs.

"If there were an Oscar for earthling suit know-how," the douche says, sitting at a desk in the corner of the room, "I'd blow the competition out of the water."

He's wearing a black outfit, only his is not like mine; for one, he's got this gray T-shirt underneath that's, you know, actually kind of cool looking. Of course, I'd never tell him that.

Meanwhile, I'm all, moving the arms and shit, "How'd you fix it?"

"Necessity," he says, his teeth sparkling, "is the mother of invention."

"Why the fuck am I wearing a tuxedo?"

"This evening, my crass little fellow, we are going to a movie premiere. This way, I can introduce you to my agent and hopefully my publicist."

"Wait—what day is it?"

"Who cares what day it is?"

"I made a date with Zoë!"

"Please. Trust me, you go back and tell this Zoë that you got cast in a feature, she'll be yours forever. Chicks love actors. At least, the paid kind. Oh—by the way," he says, turning a key into a slot on a green box of compartments, "while you were out, I managed to take a look at your penis."

Am all, "Thanks." Meanwhile, a black bug floats past the other side of the window that appears to be underwater. "Wait—you *what?*"

"You ain't lying," he says, "it's pretty prodigious, man."

"Why'd you look at it?"

"For risk of sounding like a homosexual . . . I won't use the 'c' word."

"What the fuck is the 'c' word?"

"Curious. By the way, do you know who Marlon Brando is?"

"No."

"Well, my naïve little friend, you are going to be the next Brando—an actor with balls *and* a vagina."

According to the colloquilator, a "vagina" is *something that could disrupt or stall your mission and you therefore should avoid at all costs.*

"A vagina sounds dangerous," I say.

The douche is rattling with laughter now. "What I mean is, an actor who's not afraid to reveal his feminine side."

"But I have a big dick!"

"I'm not talking about dicks. Jesus, you're really short-sighted, you know that? Look, don't process this stuff now. Just trust that when I get through with you, your work will *transcend* the box office dollars and *penetrate* the viewers' hearts like a diamond bullet."

"I don't know," I say, "that sounds like it weighs heavy on the douche scale."

Inside I can see that he's compact, spinning slowly around in these yellow dots—which means he's either so good at lying or he's simply telling the truth.

"Heh heh," he says, rubbing a towel over a small device and then placing it into this green, plastic thing that's full of square compartments.

"Wait, how'd you fix the suit?"

"You're welcome, by the way."

"Thanks."

"I've been living on this planet for so long now that I've learned a thing or two about my own suit. Yours is a *little* more advanced, but nothing beyond my unearthly intelligence. I think you swallowed something you shouldn't have. Can you think back on all that you shoved into your mouth?"

I'm all, "I had salmon with Zoë."

"Hmm . . . that wouldn't do it. Something more synthetic. Did you have McDonald's? I made that mistake once."

"No."

"Anyway, something to ponder over time. I'd *really* like to know." The douche smiles at me, his molecules inside him all green. "It's really liberating, by the way, to talk to a fellow being. You're like my new little brother."

"I'm not your brother!"

"Ho-hum."

I'm all of a sudden noticing this little, like, raised line of skin below his eye, and I'm all, "What's that, like, below the eye portion of your suit?"

"Ah! Clad you noticed, my friend. It's what they call a 'scar.' As I was saying, I've become rather equipped in modifying my suit. You see, I have to age or else I'll, you know, cause how shall I say . . . alarm? So. Over the years I've modified some of my facial features."

Suddenly, inside his suit his molecules begin to rattle, flattening out so that they form a thin line—usually it means some sadness for the past. "I'm afraid," he's saying, "I'm what some might call *über*-recognizable. Household name, that sort of stuff. You see, Clint, no matter what role I choose, audience goers only see *me*."

He smiles so big his eyes, like, expand.

Am feeling sorry for him again. Fuck. Don't know why, but am thinking I should do something stupid so that he'll keep thinking I'm an idiot. Am all, looking at these metal devices he's got laid out on this platform, "Tools!"

"By the way," he says, "don't talk like that tonight. They'll think you have Tourette's. Oh—and your name isn't Clint. Your resemblance to Eastwood is too uncanny. Of which, I have to say, they did a remarkable job. You truly are the younger Clint Eastwood incarnate. Congratulations."

"Wait. Where are we?"

"Pool house. Bottom floor. Used to be Frank Sinatra's house, you know. He was a member of what was known as the Rat Pack—look him up sometime. There's a shooting range down around here too, but I don't use it. Anyway, this window comes in handy, especially during parties where the honeys are liquored up enough to jump into the pool. It's quite a sight when one of them goes in the raw." He smiles, his teeth all sparkling as he says, "As it were."

I don't know what he's talking about, but I'm, like, imagining Zoë's face again and finding myself saying, "So if I become an actor, like, Zoë will make love to me and stuff?"

"Uh—she and half the population of the honeys on Earth."

"Honeys?"

"Earthling, American nomenclature for a rather attractive woman. Don't worry, I can teach you this stuff, Clint." The douche shuts the compartments, wiping his hands portions together. Then, his eyes blinking really fast, he's all, "Oh! Almost forgot. I came up with your new name. Your new identity. Ready? Jack."

I think about this. "Jack Eastwood?"

"Jack *Copper*."

"I don't know, it's—"

"You think it's . . . douche-esque?"

"Douche what?"

"Of course, your age group is critical for the sake of being critical. You wouldn't like any name I gave you." Inside his molecules form a sort of white web. He's frustrated. "Personally," he's saying, moving hair from his face, "I think it speaks to the oh . . . more *rugged* time in the history of the American male, before Oprah and emo bands and what have you. Back when a man was a *man*. Very *Easy Rider*, you know. Actually, who am I kidding? You don't know. Anyhow, I came up with Jack Copperson at first, but too on-the-nose—too Jack Nicholson."

I just stare at him.

"You truly are a naïve little being, aren't you?"

"No I'm not," I say, feeling stupid.

"Well, Jack Copper, let's go out into the polluted earthling air, shall we? Besides, I want to take a look at the way you walk."

The douche tells me to walk in the grass by the pool. Then, after I'm doing this, he's all, "You walk like an old lady."

"Whatever!" But now I'm thinking of all the earthlings who saw me walk, and am suddenly feeling stupid. He has me say dumb things, like, "How now brown cow," and then he's telling me I talk funny, and I'm all, shrinking inside, "Earthlings have been saying that." He reaches into the mouth portion of my suit and starts adjusting shit; then tells me that, while it's still "a little off," it should do the trick. "Say something."

"Something," I say, thinking he'll laugh. But he doesn't.

"You no longer talk out the side of your mouth, but there's traces of it. That'll be your flaw. Brando was known for his mumbling, you know. Anyway, take a seat."

I sit down on the chaise lounge chair while he walks along the pool, his molecules all blue and happy and shit. "You know, I almost figured out how to walk on water."

"Why the fuck would you want to walk on water?"

"I think I got distracted with a film and gave up. Anyway, you're going to be an anti-star, Jack Copper."

Yeah, whatever the fuck that means. Through the few palm trees, watching the lights all flicker, it's hard to imagine that maybe Zoë and Kip are one of those cars driving along a road. In fact, it's hard to imagine any of the lights, for some reason, are earthlings. Guess it's hard to imagine I'm even sitting on the Earth right now.

"So," the douche is saying, touching his shoe, like, onto the water, "like I said, you'll be meeting my agent and potentially my publicist. In order to launch your career, you'll have to impress them. But don't worry—they won't expect much. In fact, don't say much. Let your looks do most of the talking. Oh, and uh—as for your background, you were raised on a farm in Nebraska. Your parents were very reticent. Your father a rage-aholic. Your mother an alcoholic. In fact, your mother was such a lush that you used to impersonate farm animals to cheer her up. Hence your tumultuous relationship with acting, blah blah blah. Regardless, you don't speak much. We clear?"

For some reason I don't want to, like, tell him I'm clear.

"We clear?"

"Whatever."

"Excellent!"

He jumps into the air so that he lands onto the chaise lounge chair next to mine, and like that, two douches sitting there all quiet, we watch the lights flickering below.

"Want to hear something I've never told a single being," he says, pressing his hair away from his face, his molecules turning pink, "I once accidentally killed an earthling."

"You *did*?"

"It's just . . . it's . . ."

"What?"

"It's so strange to tell another being."

"Who?"

"Huh?"

"Who did you, like—kill?"

"Oh. A gaffer."

Inside, his molecules have suddenly shrunken into a tiny, gray ball, and it looks like he's almost about to cry. It's weird, am feeling all bad for him again. "Wait," I find myself saying, "what's a gaffer?"

"An earthling who handles all the lighting on a film set. It was my first film. You know, I was having so much trouble at that point with my suit, kind of like what you're going through but much worse, trust me. I'd have days where I couldn't move my legs."

"Really?"

"Sure. But I couldn't tell anyone around me."

"Totally!"

"I don't have to tell you how isolating it is. But I had instincts. I *refused* to give up. That, and I just was never affected by the rejections, like so many young actors. Fear of failure, by the way, Jack Copper, is what separates earthlings who succeed from those who fail. That's it. That's the key to success on Earth. Good things come to those who don't fear."

"Like, winners?" I say, thinking I sound cool.

"Anyway, we were filming inside what's known as a sound stage at Universal, and this piece of track lighting on the ceiling of the set kept falling. Every time these lights fell, these tiny halogen lights would shatter all over the floor—this during my scene, of course. My first real love scene. So you can imagine my apprehension. I mean, what did *I* know of earthling love at that point? Not a drop. Anyhow, the last time this little piece slipped free, a halogen light fell onto my head. And you have to believe me when I say that I was in such a state of duress and anxiety that I shouted something in our language . . . purely accidental. Frustration aimed at no one in particular. Needless to say—the gaffer fell to the floor. Flat. Like an invisible hand had ripped his heart out."

His molecules have formed into silver bubbles that are expanding throughout the suit. "The doctors," he's saying, "couldn't decide if his brain was electrocuted or if he'd died of an aneurism. I became so depressed afterward, I . . . I barely had the energy to walk, much less finish the picture. Of course, I anonymously sent all kinds of money to the gaffer's family—but let's face it, Copper, all the money on Earth can't replace an earthling."

I watch him watching the lights below, face portion of his suit all pavement solid. I find myself saying, "But—you tried."

"Yeah," he laughs, "I suppose. Anyway—it's time to go." Inside the silver bubbles have begun to form green stems of molecules. "Well, Jack Cooper," he's saying, getting up from the chair, "Hollywood is an *awfully* impatient being. We don't want to keep her waiting."

"Ever been in a Porsche?" the douche asks, putting "sunglasses" on his face even though darkness has all shown up. "Of course you haven't," he says as we're, like, driving backward out of the driveway. The thing is so red and shiny an earthling can lick its sides without getting a disease. Suddenly we're driving so fast the trees are melting into what appears to be green wires of water flying over us. I like going fast. In fact, I'm thinking I'll buy a "Porsche" when I return to Venice and drive Zoë around in it.

"So," he's asking, the hand of his suit squeezing a bar that appears to control the speed of the car, "what do you *want* from life?"

"I wanted," I say in our language, "to go on the mission, you know, for the adventure of it all."

"Speak in earthling English."

"Sorry."

"Are you saying you're nothing more than an errand boy sent by grocery clerks?"

"That's like the douchiest thing I've ever heard."

"First off, it's from a brilliant movie. Secondly, your overuse of the douche word is grating on my nerves. And—as you know, I don't even have nerves."

"Wait," I say, watching the trees blurring into the road lamps, "what if I can't act?"

"You've been acting like an earthling ever since you arrived."

"I have?"

"Do you realize how many actors in this town would *kill* to travel to a foreign planet in another fucking galaxy and *act* like one of their own?"

"I guess."

"You guess . . . well, does this Zoë think you're an earthling?"

"Yes."

"You know, Brando said that every single one of us is an actor. Look, you see a woman at work. You think she's wearing the ugliest dress on the planet. What do you tell her?"

"That the dress is fucking ugly?"

"No!" The car stops all of a sudden, and the douche waves to another earthling in a car, and then the engine's roaring as we're moving again.

"I don't really know what 'work' is."

"I'm speaking theoretically," he says, and then the car starts flashing down the hill when he's all, "Douche."

"You're the douche."

He uses his hand to hit me in the shoulder portion. "I'm just kidding, man." The douche is all smiles now. Then his smile fades and he's all talking about Brando again: "Brando was a artistic volcano of violent and complex emotions . . . at once *explosive* and feminine."

"But he was an earthling."

"Wrong!"

"He was from another planet?"

"No, he was an earthling, but one who *transcended* all Earth beings!"

"So if we're not, like, earthlings—why compare us to this Brando being?"

"You know Brando hated acting," the douche is saying, looking at himself through the small mirror, "he despised it, considered acting a lower form of art. You, Jack Copper, are going to be the same. You're a rebel with one cause—to not give a *fuck*! Plus, with my connections and experience, we'll soar above and beyond all this commercial vehicle crap."

Meanwhile, his being inside the suit has formed into several brown cubes—which, on our planet represents anger and shit. I'm all, "Why are you angry?"

"I'm not angry," he says, his eyes widening as he smiles.

"Wait," I say, "did any being ever wonder about your real, like, identity?"

"Once," he says as we stop beside a pink house that appears to have been built upside down, "on my way into the Fox lot I encountered a little trouble. But their security's impossible. Anyway, Jack Copper, whereas the trajectory of my career aimed toward fame, yours will point toward the cosmos. Which is to say I'm going to groom you to partake only in serious, gut-wrenching roles, independent films—films that capture the human spirit. Don't worry, I won't let you—"

Something beeps.

The douche reaches into his jacket, retrieves a phone device, and says, "Speak."

We've stopped on a road lined with palm trees that seem to be trying with all their strength to reach the pink clouds.

Next to us, two females in a car have also stopped. And now they're staring at the douche, their necks filling with black tongues.

"I know you," the female driver says to the douche.

"Nice to see you," the douche says, smiling. Then he's all covering his mouth with a hand. "Ask them for a blow job."

"A what?"

"Just do it!"

According to the colloquilator, a "blow job" *is a form of sodomy, which, in many sectors on Earth, is illegal.*

"Go ahead," he's saying, "hurry up, before the light changes."

"No. You're trying to, like, trick me."

"So you're afraid of a blow job now?"

"No . . . I don't know."

"Good things come to those who don't fear, Jack Copper."

"Shut up!"

"Yeah," the douche says, "you're a real rebel."

Whatever. I turn to the female driver and say, "Can I have a job blow?"

"What?" The girl laughs.

"Blow job, dummy. Ask them for a *blow job*."

"Blow job," I say.

The females look at each other, and then the one driving is all, "Maybe—what's your name?"

"Say Jack Copper."

"Jack Copper," I say.

Suddenly, our car launches forward and we're driving so fast for a second it feels like we're about to hit a patch of darkness.

"Was that so difficult?"

"What's a blow job?"

"Those girls are willing to suck on your dick just because I'm famous."

"Really?"

"'Tis a shame what an earthling won't do for wealth and fame."

Now I'm all curious and shit to see if more earthlings are going to look at us. Then this earthling in a black car the size of a house looks down at the douche, and when the douche looks up at him, the earthling makes a strange sign with his two fingers. Which, the douche totally returns. "Peace sign," the douche says, driving forward again and manipulating the engine with that control stick, "though most earthlings have no idea what peace actually is."

"So—earthlings look at you everywhere you, like, go?"

The douche looks over at me, and inside I can see his molecules beginning to shrink a little, turning white. "Correct."

"What's that like?"

"Empty."

"Empty?"

"Look, there's nothing more . . . blah, for lack of a better word, than an earthling you've never met approaching you like he knows you and telling you how much he loves your work or your face or the dump you took after dinner last night."

"I don't get it. If they know you don't like it, why do they do it?"

"Fame is a bit of a paradox, my friend. You're only famous so long as some earthling in a gas station or wherever gawks at you. Which is why you, Mr. Copper," he says, and the car is beginning to slow down, the engine all groaning, "are going to focus on *films*— not the fame."

We turn onto a small hill surrounded by thick vegetation. "Is this the premiere thing?"

"Want to see a premiere? Turn on the television. This, Mr. Copper, is the Chateau Marmont."

An earthling with black hair and brown skin opens the door. I'm all, getting out of the car, "Thanks."

"No problem, sir," he says, filled with what looks like trees that fire has, like, eaten.

"What's wrong with him?" I ask the douche as we walk up steps.

"Working class," he says as we walk. "Hates his job. Doesn't own a thing. Swimming in debt. Only the wealthy need apply, Jack Copper. Welcome to the United States of America."

An earthling male and female walk past us dressed like us, both of them staring at the douche. He smiles at them, and then is all, "Remember what we said about your background?"

"That I'm from Brenaska?"

"Good enough," he says, moving his hair away from his face.

We're walking past a pool, like, out of which a female earthling, wearing only two tiny pieces of red cloth, steps, her nipples portion of her breasts all stiff and shit underneath the cloth. Meanwhile, white tongues erupt when she notices the douche, a smile expanding on her face.

Suddenly a black earthling, surrounded by several black earthlings, dips his head in a strange fashion as he approaches us. "What up, son?"

The douche is all, "What up, Snoop?"

"You know," the black earthling says, "kickin' it."

"Aight," the douche says.

The black earthlings continues moving past the pool. But they weren't filled with tongues. I'm all, "What's wrong with them?"

"Nothing." The douche laughs. "Why?"

"They weren't, like, fond of you."

"That's because he's also talent."

We're walking up a hill of steps now that lead us into more vegetation, all kinds of trees so thick it's like we've entered a different planet. "That reminds me," the douche says, turning around as we, like, reach the top step, "you're an anarchist who hates acting."

"I am?"

"Yes."

"But I don't know how to act."

"Which is *exactly* why they're going to love you."

"That makes no fucking sense."

The douche expands inside, turning into red cubes. "Listen up, Copper, and listen good, okay?"

"I guess."

"Don't guess!"

His red cubes are beginning to form one giant cube. Uh-oh. Am suddenly worried he's going to, like, throw me down the stairs. Still, I can't help but say, "Then don't tell me what to do."

"Okay," he says, looking around, "that's rebellious, I guess. Work with that. In the meantime, listen to me. And listen good. Movies. TV. Intellectual property, what have you—it's all product, okay?"

"Okay," I say, watching the flickering lights down the hill, not wanting to look into his eyes.

"Look at me."

"Okay!"

"Now. Imagine every single talent in this town is a kilo of cocaine. Got it? Having said that, my product is becoming a little . . . oh, difficult to move, so to speak. Everyone and his mother's had a taste.

Which is mostly my fault for eagerly making blockbuster choices and—anyway, you, Jack Copper, on the other hand, are the new drug in town."

"I am?"

"Yes."

I'm all, trying to imagine myself a gigantic needle or something, "Wait—how can I be a drug?"

"A drug no one's had the pleasure of tasting."

"What the fuck is that supposed to mean?"

"Don't question it!"

"Okay . . . but it just sounds stupid."

"Rebellion is one thing. Questioning everything like a child is annoying."

"And saying everything like a . . ." I can't think of what to say. Besides, I'm growing all angry; now *my* molecules forming into a cube. Then I'm watching the lights flickering on the flat land below; and when I turn back the douche has already begun ascending the path. And I find myself saying, "No!"

"Excuse me?"

"Acting like a drug is—it's not me."

He walks down so that he's standing over me. "Don't be an idiot, Copper."

"I'm not Jack Copper. Stop calling me that."

"I'm afraid you are now, my friend."

"I'm not your friend. You know what, I don't want to act. I just decided. Fuck it! I don't want to do it."

Inside his suit, each of his molecules expands into a red planet with white and blue wires twisting and shit. He grabs my head portion. Then spins it so that I'm facing down at the pool.

I'm all, "What're you doing?"

"Just stay still."

"Stop!" I say, but I can't break free. Then he sticks a finger inside the ear portion of my suit so far I suddenly can't move. I go to speak and I can't. Then he releases. Lets go of me and . . .

I'm suddenly running down the steps, shouting, "I can run! I can *run!*"

I get to the bottom of the steps. Molecules vibrating so fast I can't stop. Then I'm running over the pool.

It's just so fucking freeing to run that I'm all running across the pool the other way now—female watching me from a chair—and then running up the steps so fast I'm suddenly loving everything on the Earth at once!

"Did you see me run?" I say to the douche when I get to the top. "Did you see?"

"Yes," he says, smiling, "very impressive."

"Fuck yeah, it was."

Being vibrating so fast now I want to do it again. "I'm going again." But he grabs my arm portion and is all, "All right, Copper, there's plenty of time for that later. Now. This is your moment. Are you ready?"

Molecules are vibrating; wanting to run. In fact, I want to run down the steps. Out into the road. And see if I can, like, stop a car. Am all, "I'm ready for anything."

An earthling with black hair in a black suit has just emerged from a little house and now stands before us, looking me up and down, a blue tongue flapping inside him. "Did this motherfucker just walk on water?"

"Dan," the douche says, "Jack Copper. Jack Copper, my agent."

"Christ," the agent says, smiling as he reaches his hand out to touch me, "note to self: I've got to stop taking sleeping pills. Other day, I drove halfway to work in my pajamas. I'm working too much, my man. Anyway—nice to meet you, Jack."

"Fuck acting," I find myself saying.

"Have him," the agent says to the douche, "in my office first thing on Monday morning."

"Done," says the douche, smiling so big it's like his sparkly teeth are burning lightbulbs.

My being is beating faster and faster—I want to run so fast and then leap into the air like a bird. "Can I run again? Can I? Can I?"

"Not yet," he says.

Question: If I fly into the clouds, will I just float into space?

I start running down the steps when the douche grabs my arm portion, and then we're entering this little house that's, like, built into the hill, covered in vegetation—all lit up inside.

On the couch an earthling with hair like Kip holds on to his head like he's trying to pull it off. Other male earthlings stand around the room, drinking from glasses.

"The fuck is he?" the earthling on the couch says, lighting a cigarette. Meanwhile, I have way too much energy for this boring room. Then I see a blue light flickering behind that earthling's eye, and I'm all—wait, is this earthling, like, angry with *me*? "Jack Copper," I say, "who the *fuck* are you?"

"Are you fucking kidding me, dude?"

"You," I say, feeling like I can throw him off the planet, "some sort of movie *pro-doucher*?"

"The fuck he just call me?" the earthling says, looking at the other males around the room. A silver-haired earthling starts staring at me like he wants to kiss me.

"You going to intro-douche me," I say. The agent starts rattling with laughter. "I love this kid."

"I hate him," the earthling on the couch says. Smoke in his body turns all yellow. And he's just staring at me. So I'm all, "Do I look like a bitch?"

"Yeah," he says, pressing his cigarette into an ashtray, "you do."

"Wait—you're supposed to, like, say no."

"Loser."

"I'm a winner!"

"Okay," the silver-haired earthling laughs, "we're all friends here."

"Does he look like anyone?" the douche asks.

"Wait a second," the agent says, "wait . . ."

"Young dirty hairy," the silver-haired earthling says.

"Holy fuck!" says the earthling on the couch, smoke leaking out of his stupid mouth. "He does."

"Clint Eastwood in his teens," the douche says, looking around the room, "can I pick 'em or what?"

I hate this room and I want to run back to Venice and see if I can, like, run onto the surface of the ocean. And then go find Zoë and make love to her. I find myself jumping into the air. Up and down.

I hear laughter. So I decide to, like, walk on my hands. Why not? But when I'm all upside down, staring at the black shoes of these earthlings my molecules begin to fall and all that energy is—

Gone.

And I'm falling to the floor . . . and beginning, to, like, melt . . .

The douche and I are driving light-speed again under the pink, flickering sky in his Porsche. "I'm *very* proud of you, Copper."

Meanwhile, I've fallen to the feet portion of the suit, and I can't seem to fill it. "I'm not," I manage to say, "Jack Copper. What happened to . . . my . . . suit back there?"

The douche is laughing; the engine roaring.

I look out the window to see palm trees reaching for space.

[resume log: 40.20]

Can't seem to fill suit.

Darkness invaded completely. Still in douche's Porsche.

Appear to have stopped in foreign wooden section. No houses around.

"Let me explain a little about the world of Hollywood, Jack Copper."

Am losing vision.

"Most earthlings," he's saying, "will never experience significant change in a lifetime—except when they die, of course, or, in some cases, contract a terminable disease. You see, boys and girls, such as yourself—were you an earthling—and, in general, the audience we in the film industry target, are particularly bereft of change."

"Want," I say, my voice sounding all tired, "to go back . . . to Venice to see . . . Zoë."

"Okay, let's just say most earthlings don't change. We clear, Jack Copper? Now. You see, nothing excites an earthling more than positive change. Negative change, on the other hand, is what all earthlings fear. An earthling walks into your house and shoots your wife. Negative change. A winning lottery ticket. Positive change. You get it? Meeting the man or woman of his or her dreams. Positive, romantic change. Getting elected as president. Ending a war. Healing the sick. Feeding the poor. The list goes on. Now, you have to trust me when I say any life event that yields a positive change is rare on this earth, and when it occurs . . . well, that's one happy moment.

"Now.

"Seeing how ninety-six percent of earthlings will never change their personalities much less the outcomes of their mundane, boring lives, there are three primary aspects of society through which they can experience positive change vicariously. And they are as follows: Cinema. Politics. And sports.

"In cinema, characters are given an opportunity at the outset of the picture to change. By the end, they've transcended the pathetic, lifeless existence they'd been enduring only ninety minutes ago, when the film began.

"In sports, a team wins—positive change. In politics, voters affect change and so forth.

"So that is why, Mr. Jack Copper, you were here tonight. To affect change among all these desperately bored earthlings. Got that? Oh, who am I kidding? Of course you do!"

Am contracting . . . douche's being has expanded into orange balls so bright he's glowing inside, and I'm thinking I've never seen that before in one of our beings when he's all, "You feel that?"

"What?" I say, trying with all my strength to fill the suit.

"The earth. You feel it move just now?"

Can't move.

"Did you feel it jolt just now?"

Must focus.

"Did you feel the ground shake?"

"Please take me to . . . Venice. I . . . don't . . . like you."

"Did you hear that?"

"Shut . . . up."

"Do you realize in the time I started rambling on about all change, that across Earth several hundred earthlings have died?"

"Stop . . ."

"And guess what, Jack Copper? Earth could care less. It just

keeps revolving around the sun without a single care in the world—
heh heh—for a single one of its inhabitants."

The douche is inserting a finger into the nose portion of my suit,
and I'm trying to fill the suit to stop him, but it's just . . . too . . .
much—

[????]

Electric eye staring at me. Black stripes that keep disappearing and reappearing beyond eye . . . where am I?

[????]

Electric eye, staring at me again. The suit's open, I know it. Can't move a single molecule. Father, I am sorry for not . . .

[????]

Still can't move.

Can't react. Can only think. Can't seem to access number of cycles for log.

Captured by darkness.

Must be traveling back to planet, hitting a great big pocket of darkness. . . . It doesn't feel that way, though. Just have my thoughts. Sucks.

Thought: If I think of nothing, I'll no longer, like, exist.

[resume log: 29.83]

I can see . . .

Myself! I can see myself! The suit. There I am.

Question: Why am I looking at my own suit?

[29.71]

I can see . . . myself walking back and forth, one of the arms now reaching toward the head to, like, touch the hair. Question: What's happened to me?

[29.49]

Thought: Someone inside my suit. Focus on moving. Can't move. Question: Where I am? When I focus on moving, I lose my vision. . . . Fuck!

[29.38]

Everything has gone white. Still no idea where I am. I look for myself, in the suit—I miss seeing it. Nothing. Thoughts. Whiteness.

[28.30]

My suit is talking.

"You talkin' to me," it's saying, "you talkin' to me?"

Molecules stuck; can't move.

"Hon," I hear, "is that you?"

I see my suit crash to the floor. Something floats out of its ear. The douche!!!!

I try, like, to expand.

Nothing.

[27.66]

"You was my brother, Charlie," the douche is saying through my suit, "I could have had class. I could have been a *contender*. I could have been *somebody*, instead of a bum . . . which is what I am."

Trying to move one . . . molecule.

[26.44]

Appear to be stuffed inside a container. On the wall of this container is a hole so small it's like an ant made it.

It's this hole I've been watching the douche through all this time. He stuffed my molecules into a small container. He's got me captured. Question: Why?

"Who do you think you are?" my suit says.

The douche has taken over my suit! Question: Why?

Suddenly, like he heard my thoughts, my suit walks over to the container I'm in, and then I see the face—the young Clint Eastwood!—the nose coming at me, and I freeze. Don't move. Don't think.

The face leaves.

[26.21]

Thought: He's stealing the suit so that he can use it to become a different actor!

Fuck. I'm such an idiot for trusting him! Father, I have failed! Question: Why can't I still move? Must be strong. Focus. Concentrate. Can't.

Fuck.

No. Like douche said, no fear. Am thinking of Father. Of Zoë. Of Kip. Every earthling I've met so far. Am thinking of the black ocean when . . .

Molecules quiver.

"Yes!"

Oops. Have to remain quiet.

[25.74]

Imagining that I'm under the ocean—angry wave slapping at me when . . . another molecule moves.

138

Am beginning to expand and contract a little. Container tiny—size of an earthling finger.

Am expanding still . . .

[23.17]

Am out!

The small, black canister rolls off the shelf and falls onto the wooden platform. Uh-oh.

Darkness. No light in the room.

Light inside the pool—water all white through the round window . . .

Scanning room for suit. Don't see it. Not good. Must find. Must not fear. Must focus.

Hear sounds like the ocean. What?

Female earthling swims past the window. It's Karen, the douche's wife!

She swims past again when I discover she's naked. Fistful of red hair between her legs . . . pink "nipples" on her breasts. Colloquilator still working. Such beautiful creatures, these earthlings!

Hair flaps in the water, looking like something that grew out from the bottom of the ocean.

Thought: Should slip into the douche's suit and make love to her. She'll never know. No. Need to find Zoë.

Drift about the room, scanning for suit.

Another wave sound. Ah! My suit—young Clint Eastwood—

swims past the window, all naked, big stupid dick swaying in the water between its legs.

"The douche!"

My suit floats in the middle of the water; I see Karen's body float up next to it. Her legs wrap around the legs of my suit. Am hovering in the corner of the room. Thought: Think!

[23.10]

Somebeing walking downstairs. Am contracting, floating near the little container that's fallen off the shelf.

Naked, my suit walks into the room. Without bothering to turn on the light, I see the douche slip out the ear of the suit . . . his being is all yellow and green molecules, now floating out of the room so fast it's like he's afraid.

[22.97]

Am slipping into the suit.

Moving arms.

Moving legs. Testing mouth.

"How now brown cow." It works!

Ascend steps . . . slowly.

Standing outside. Ocean of lights flickering below. Looking down at penis portion. Oops.

Descending steps.

Scanning room for clothing.

Ah! Tuxedo all folded up next to what appears to be a black rubber suit.

Must get away from the douche and be safe. . . .

Ascending the stairs. Am outside.

[pause]

Something's different about the house in Venice. One, the "carpet" is on fire. Two, hundreds of earthlings, most of them filled with toxic substances, are drinking out of cans and bottles.

"Where's Zoë?" I ask a shirt-free earthling. He's all, swallowing beer, "Who?"

Another earthling is pouring beer onto flames on the carpet while others laugh.

Fuck it, I'm going to babble the truth to Zoë about everything. I don't care about anything anymore. Going upstairs, while the earthlings fill their bodies with toxins beneath me, I'm still all angry I allowed the douche to totally trick me. I simply don't even know what's true.

Maybe earthling love will, like, cure my thoughts.

Instead of Zoë, a female earthling smokes a cigarette by the window. I'm watching the smoke enter her body and escape when she's all, "Is something burning downstairs?"

Am all, "No," thinking from now on I'm responding with short answers and shit.

Then I find myself babbling: "It was. But someone, like, poured beer on it."

"You're an actor, right?"

Her hair is the color of pavement; her eyes like grass. "You know," I find myself saying, "your eyes are like grass and your hair is like pavement."

"I've never heard that one before," she laughs. Inside her a pink flower grows so that its petals fill up her entire body. Am thinking I should look for Zoë, but can't stop looking at this flower inside her.

"So what's with the tux?"

"Chateau," I say, "Marmont."

"Okay, now I know where I've seen you," she's saying. "You were on that sitcom about the . . . when you were younger, right, like, ten years ago?"

"I am Jack Copper."

"Hmm . . . sounds familiar."

She is wearing a "skirt" that's short enough where I can see little marks on her thighs. As I get closer, I see that the marks are small, brown specs. "You have freckles," I say, pointing at her leg.

"You know," she says, "when I was little, I used to try to peel them off."

She touches my arm and says, "You don't have any freckles—hey wow, you must work out, like, *all* the time."

Work out? Stupid colloquilator!

She reaches out and touches the shoulder portions of my suit and inside I expand to the point where the suit suddenly, like, pauses . . . and then I'm falling back onto the bed and she, like, joins me. The suit begins to sweat, the tuxedo pants getting all wet. I remove them, and am starting to remove the white shirt when she's all, "Oh, my God, you're body is—wow."

"What?"

Lying on the bed, staring up at her freckles and shit, I'm thinking it's finally going to happen. In fact, I'm trying not to think. Forget thinking. Now her face is all serious, like she's about to kill me. Without saying anything she, like, starts opening up her shirt by manipulating these small, plastic round things.

Freckles are, like, scattered all over her skin. Smiling now, she removes her bra. Her breasts are staring at me—two pink eyes.

Suddenly, my dick, like, stands up. Am all, "I'm sorry it's so big."

"Aren't you Mr. Modest?"

"Who?"

"Oh, my God—you ain't joking."

Inside I start to, like, quiver, my entire suit shaking, sweat flooding the chest area now. It's going to happen! I'm experiencing earthling love! It must happen! She leans down and kisses the penis. My molecules contract . . . and then expand so fast I almost lose vision.

"Ouch," she says, staring up at me, "I just got shocked."

"Sorry."

"It's okay," she says, grabbing the dick, "it's kind of hot."

This orange light erupts between her legs, it's like the color of the sun when it falls into the water.

Suddenly, like I can't control it, the hand of the suit reaches up and grabs her breast, and she says, "Mmm . . . God it tickles—you have such a strange touch!" She then starts using her tongue to wipe my neck dry from sweat. Each time her tongue touches my suit I begin to blink.

Am blinking, like faster and faster. Am starting to lose vision.

Then gaining vision.

Then seeing Zoë standing by the door.

Uh-oh.

"Hi?" I say to Zoë.

The female earthling smiles all weirdly, with my dick in her hand. And inside her that light disappears, and it's replaced by these gray dots.

It's so good to see Zoë! Yet, inside I can see that she's full of something bad—this red thing growing into what looks like a pole.

"Clint," she says, breathing all heavy now, "this was, like, our bed. How could you do this to me?"

"Zoë!"

I climb off the bed, and then follow Zoë downstairs and outside, and onto Speedway, where the homefree earthlings are gone, probably 'cause they're in our house, and then onto the beach, where

Zoë's running toward the black waves that I can hear crashing. She's running so fast I can't keep up. In fact, I can't run. Can't figure out how the douche had manipulated my suit to run and act all crazy for a few moments. I fall to the sand. I get up and try again. I fall. So I do my best to walk fast toward her, but it's too late . . . she disappears over the horizon.

"Asshole!" the woman who said I work out a lot yells. She's now standing on the paved path along the beach.

"What's an asshole?" I yell back. According to the colloquilator, an "asshole" is *a crude term for the sphincter portion of an earthling.*

"You really think I'm, like, a gigantic asshole?" I say, but she's already returned inside.

Meanwhile, earthlings walk by on the paved path, laughing at me. It's then I realize all I'm wearing is this douchey bow tie. And my stupid penis is, like, still stiff.

No wonder, I'm thinking, the words "human" and "humiliation" sound the same. It's, like, totally impossible, this attempt to be human. . . .

14

Moon hangs over black ocean, turning water all silver and shit.

I like the moon—takes away some of the darkness. No earthlings walking on beach in darkness.

Thought: Maybe earthlings always afraid 'cause each evening, whether they like it or not, they're forced to, like, deal with darkness. Douche talked about "positive change" and shit. Maybe earthlings afraid to change 'cause the stupid Earth is all changing around them all the time. The light. The darkness. The waves. The moon.

Meanwhile, all angry, ocean groans as its water spills along sand, almost until it reaches the toes portion of my suit . . . only to recede into the mass of darkness again.

Question: What about the mission?

Answer: Don't know what's right.

[20.40]

Am looking into the blackness of ocean; I am not winning on this earth.

Question: Is there a fear-free place somewhere? Probably. Follow-up: Does it cost money to enter it?

Walking away from the water so that it can't swallow me.

Question: Is it wrong to make earthling love to a different female other than "your girl"? Answer: Am thinking most definitely *yes*.

Sucks. Zoë's all sad. I'm sad.

Question: Am I doomed 'cause I let the douche fool me?

At wooden umbrellas section near Speedway when I hear, "My *man* . . . naked as the day is long."

[pause]

"Son, where in God's name are your motherfucking clothes?"

"In the house, Carl."

"Is that a bow tie?" Carl laughs forever, it seems. When he's done, I'm all, "I don't know, like . . . sort of."

"You know if you don't wear no clothes, the police might take your ass in for the night?" Carl grabs this big gray blanket from his shopping cart, and then, like, hangs it on my back. Inside his head I no longer see that crazy cluster of electronic activity, but that's probably 'cause I suck at sensing.

Am all, "You want money, Carl?"

"Son, I always want money." Then Carl's laughing again. "But something tells me you ain't got none on you."

"I ain't got none," I tell Carl, and then I'm all finding myself saying, "I hurt Zoë, Carl."

"Son, let me tell you something about women. Whatever you did, no matter how bad you think it is, she will forgive you. Women—they nurturing all the time, even when mad. It's in they blood. As long as you're sorry for what you did, a woman will always forgive. Now, you a nice boy—shit, you an angel, maybe. I doubt you hurt her all that bad."

"This one female had her hand on my dick, like, when Zoë walked in."

Carl begins to rub his face. "Son, forget everything I just said. You fucked."

"Am I, like, doomed?"

"Guess you can say that."

"How do I, like, fix myself?"

"Only the good Lord can set you free. And then, and only then, maybe Zoë, too, will forgive you. By the way, I've been taking meds, thanks to you."

"Med? Wait, how do I find this . . . lord?"

"God lives inside all of us."

"That sucks."

"Why?"

"I was kind of, like, hoping he'd live in a place where I could talk to him, you know, ask questions and shit."

Carl takes a seat on the bench, and once again begins to rub his face so hard it makes me wonder if he's got some disease in his brain. Inside I can see him turning all white and orange, confusion maybe? Now I'm, like, not sure of my senses.

"What you need," he's saying, "is a church, a great big church to set yourself right once and for all. God can heal you, son. But I know for damn sure you already an angel. Well, after what you just did . . . maybe not." Carl smiles all big and says, "You one of them angels come down here to test me. Boy I know that."

"Where do I find a church?"

"Well, that there's a trick question."

"What the fuck is that supposed to mean?"

"Son, God is everywhere."

"Then how the fuck will I know what a church is?"

"For an angel, you got a mouth on you—maybe you're the devil, I don't know. Look, you'll know a church when you see lots of people going in, and peaceful people coming out on Sunday— God's day."

God has a day? Strange. Am all, "Thanks, Carl," and start walking.

[resume log: 19.86]

Am walking along a street in sector that appears to be full of stores, sidewalks made from a different material than ones in Venice; sidewalks so clean an earthling could "lick" them without catching disease. Been walking along street called Monica Santa. No sign of God. No church.

Thought: Church will open when sunlight returns.

[19.20]

Sector appears to host, like, only rich earthlings. All stores closed. No homefree earthlings anywhere. Gigantic lamps are on. Earthlings divided into ones who work—ones who don't. Homefree and the homefull. Homefull call the homefree "bums." Homefree call the homefull "slaves." Question: Is there a sector on Earth where no one, like, works?

Question for God: If they just got rid of money altogether, would Earth be at peace?

[18.93]

Red and blue lights flashing against windows of the store.

Turn to see electric eye shining at me. "Police!" I find myself saying. Uh-oh. Must run.

Don't know how to run.

Thought: Police can capture me and cut me open.

Am sticking finger portion into ear, trying to find the thing the douche had pushed. Meanwhile, the car is talking: "Sir," says car, "what happened to your clothes?"

I remove finger from ear and then give them "the peace sign."

Car is all, "Sir, do you realize it's illegal to walk around naked?"

Am all, "I have a blanket."

Car follows all slow like as I keep walking. Behind window is black shoes under light.

"Sir, is that a bow tie around your neck?" Two earthlings wearing blue clothing step out of the car.

Inside am beginning to expand, wanting to escape. Question: How do I get free of these policelings? Behind window stands this dead earthling male dressed in a red pants and shirt. What the—? Good thing I can see out from any area of the suit. Policelings have no idea I'm watching them as I, like, walk.

"Ain't it a little cold, sir," says one, "to not be wearing clothes on this lovely brisk evening?" Other one laughs.

Thought: Do something an earthling would never do. Scare them. Lowering head portion behind me so that it's, like, hanging upside down and facing them as I walk all forward.

"Hello," I say to them all upside down.

"Holy fuck," one says, "he some kind of yoga freak?"

"What did you take tonight, sir?"

"He's probably just triple-jointed. I've seen that on Discovery."

"Sir, why don't you stop walking, okay?"

"Do you know where you are, sir?"

"Am looking for a church," I say, returning with all my strength to normal position.

"Churches are closed, sir."

One policeling filled inside with little, like, seashells all rattling.

"Let's just take him down."

"Oh man, it's not even worth the paperwork."

"Sir, is it *really* necessary for you to resist arrest?"

"Sir, if you keep walking, we have reason to believe you're up to

no good tonight. So why don't you stop and we'll have a little chat.
How's that sound, huh?"

Exiting the suit . . .

Hovering above policelings. Am now watching as suit falls and
crashes onto clean sidewalk, arms and legs all spread out.

Expanding.

Uh-oh.

Occupying air over the street.

Continuing to expand . . . remembering what the douche said.
Relaxing . . .

Beginning to contract . . . into size of an earthling head. Am
hovering over policelings again. Both are filled with all these
orange balls inside.

"Dude just fell like a bag of bricks."

"I know, like he got shot, right?"

"Feel his pulse."

Thought: Can enter one like the douche entered my suit. Enter
through ear, inside policeling now . . . there is so much blood! Weird.

Beginning expansion through his body. Feeling electric sensation . . . ball of molecules in his chest resisting. Expanding with
more strength.

Feel his body let go. Have full control. Am all, through his mouth,
"Test." Worked.

Walking backward, away from other policeling and my suit.

"Frank," policeling saying, "where're you going?"

Thought: Should say something male earthling would, like, never say . . . "My period."

"Your what?" he laughs.

"My vagina . . . it hurts."

"Did you just say—Frank, we have a suspect here lying on the fucking ground. What are you saying, man?"

"I got my period today."

"What the—what the fuck is wrong with your mouth, it's—what's—"

"We can't make love 'cause of my period. Sorry."

The policeling turns white inside, and is all, walking toward me, "Listen, Frank, buddy, okay? All that shit that went down last week about that picture of your wife . . . I had *nothing* to do with that, I swear on my kids, Frank. Fuck that, I swear on my dead mother. You got to believe me, Frank. If I saw that about *my* girl I'd want to kill someone. Come on, buddy, let's just be cool . . . let's do our jobs here. A man's life is at stake."

"Okay."

"All right, Frank. We cool?"

"My vagina is cool."

"All right, all right, am I on camera here? Is this some practical joke shit? 'Cause if it's not, Frank, I'm going to have to write you up. And I'm not a rat."

Blinking light inside his head. Am saying, "How about a blow job?"

"Fuck me!" Policeling begins walking back and forth, blinking light in his head. "Maybe you should sit down, Frank. Maybe you're just . . . all right, Frank, I think someone put some acid into your coffee. You're not sounding like—man, your mouth's all moving funny. Just breathe and—I'm your boy on this, all right? Now. I'm going to take care of the suspect. Just stand there. And breathe."

He starts walking back to my suit.

Open door of police car and sit body onto seat. Several buttons. Pull down lever. Car moves forward. Other policeling running after the car, shouting, "Frank!!!"

Pressing buttons.

Lights on roof flashing, car screaming. Don't like noise. Pressing more buttons.

Car stops.

Exiting the body.

Car moving again all slowly. Other policeling now running after car. "Frank!!!"

Hover over to my suit. Reentering.

Walking into a narrow street, which I'm halfway down when I think, Alleyway!

[17.49]

Thought: Fuck church. Will apprehend douche while darkness still hovering. Will return to Venice and talk to Zoë; tell her I am sorry.

Walking along Mulholland drive now. Thought: Each time car comes, have to hide. Still wearing dumb blanket.

Meanwhile, yellow car driving very, very fast, coming at me. . . .

[17.39]

Falling down from what I think is called a "cliff."

[16.99]

Indentation under arm must have been pressed during fall. Am looking for arm portion in wooded section. Arm portion was unlocked from shoulder. First pink particles of light have returned.

[16.27]

Am locking arm.

Now standing in wooded section behind what appears to be a small house. Opposite of the douche's house—not much vegetation. No pool. Grass looks like it's been on fire.

Sunlight all spilling over trees now.

"I don't want," hear a female earthling from inside the house say, "to get there before it's too crowded!"

"In a minute!" says younger male earthling.

"What're you doing? You always need a minute. Why can't you just be ready when I say it's time to go?"

"Leave me alone, Mom!"

Thought: Maybe they're going to church.

[16.08]

Exiting suit.

Red bicycle lying on grass—must belong to the little male. Glass door appears to be open.

Drifting inside, looking for clothing.

Female activating a computer on desk. She puts her hands to the side of her head, like it's too heavy to hold; she says, "Sweetie, you ready?"

"I need ten minutes," says little male from other room.

Orange crumbs on the floor of the kitchen, and "toys" lying all over the floor in the room with the television.

Stack of clothing on couch.

Using molecules to lift black pants made of a material much lighter than the jeans. White shirt made of what appears to be stretchable material. Thought: The douche said we are visible in pure form. Uh-oh.

Female stands in kitchen now, looking into refrigerator. She has a little earthling inside the belly portion of her body. Seeing little head, tiny arms; inside tiny earthling's head what looks like a yellow plant maybe. Around baby is green, hard shell . . . around that shell full of these pointy things, anxiety? Yes. Probably why she wants to go to church.

Drift back outside. Reenter suit. Put on clothes.

[15.78]
Walking around house. Open back door of car. Crumbs lying all over red carpet. Raise legs over the head portion so that I resemble a ball.

Eventually, they enter. Car vibrates. Engine roars.

"I'm hungry," the little male is saying up front.

"What else is new?"

"My poo is new!"

"Ha-ha."

"Asshole!" says the mother. "That guy drives like Grandma."

"You ain't supposed to swear, Mom."

"I ain't, huh?"

"You *aren't* supposed to, like, swear."

"With assholes like that on the road, it's hard not to."

"I'm hungry."

"Me too."

"You're always hungry!"

"Yeah well, I'm pregnant, dummy. I'm supposed to be fat."

"Don't call me dummy."

Outside, palm trees passing by. Mother saying, "You're not a dummy, sweetie."

[15.50]

"I told you it was crowded, look at all these people," mother says as the car slows. Then she's all, "Goddamnit!"

"Who cares?"

"You know I hate that expression. I care, all right? And let me tell you something, Mister, some day you'll care about stuff, *believe* me. And you'll come to me asking for advice."

"No I won't!"

"Yes, you will."

"Won't!"

"Will!"

The doors shut. Appear to be in gigantic, dark place where cars sit.

Waiting until they've walked close enough to the church, and then I'll exit out the back door.

[15.30]

Carl said they'd all "dress nice" on Sunday. All earthlings moving toward gigantic building whose doors are electric. Earthlings moving in. On other side, earthlings exiting.

Getting closer.

Earthlings arriving are filled with black, pointy things. Anxiety. Earthlings emerging from the wide doors are filled with green fur—peace.

Ah, an earthling church. Am expanding inside the suit; excited to ask God questions and resume mission.

Question: What if God doesn't know about my planet?

[15.08]

Inside church.

Friendly-looking female earthling in brown hair and blue clothing smiling at me. Must be a being employed by God. Ah, an angel! Inside, she is full of what appears to be yellow boxes.

Am all, "Hello."

"Hello, I like your bow tie."

"Fuck!"

"Excuse me."

Must focus. Am all, "I have questions."

"Great—I have answers."

"Can you show me where God is?"

Inside her boxes turn to orange liquid, confusion? Suddenly thinking again what the douche said about me not knowing how to sense. Shit.

"Is that so?" she says, smile curling over her face.

"It is so," I tell her, thinking church earthlings talk strange. Return big smile. Both of us smiling.

Feeling douchey. Stop smiling. She must be feeling douchey too—'cause she stops smiling. "Well," she says, pointing at the metal stairs, "this is IKEA."

Earthlings pass, she smiling at them, one by one.

Am all, "IKEA."

"That's right."

"What the fuck is that supposed to mean?"

Male earthling with no hair asks her where he can locate "the couches."

"Second floor," she says, "can't miss them."

Hair-free earthling full of anxiety.

She's smiling at me again, orange liquid filling her legs and arms. "Is there something I can help you with, something IKEA-related?"

"Is IKEA . . . God?"

"IKEA *is* God!" says male earthling passing, smiling as he now ascends electronic, metal stairs.

Her body rattling with laughter. "It might be, who knows?"

"Wait, why don't you know God?"

"I beg your pardon."

"I want to speak to God—is this church?"

"Listen, I don't know what's going on with you, but—"

"I came for church."

"I'm sorry, sweetie, this isn't church." Inside she's growing with anger, that blinking light. "This is a place for furniture, and a variety of other household items. Now, if you're looking for something other than stuff for your home or office, I'm afraid we can't help you. I'm really sorry."

Am following earthlings up electronically moving stairs.

Earthling in pink shirt turns around and smiles at me, like he wants to talk. Am all, "Do you know where I can find God?"

He turns all green inside. "Not only do I know God, but I know Jesus Christ *personally*."

"Who the fuck is he?"

Blinking light behind his eyes. "Oh, you think that's funny?"

"I am here to talk to God."

"Not with a mouth like that."

"Wait, God's here?"

"God's inside all of us. Duh."

"Not me."

"Well, I can help you accept Jesus into your heart."

"I don't know . . . sounds kind of douchey."

"You know what? When you're burning in hell after you die, don't say I didn't tell you so."

Am all, in low-like voice, "Are you from Earth?"

"I came from heaven, where I'm going to return someday to be with my father."

"Heaven. Is that, like, your planet?"

"No, stupid. It's not a *planet*. Gosh, you're *really* deceived."

"I am?"

"You need healing."

"I do?"

"You have an evil sprit in you."

"I do?"

"Duh!"

Thought: If this earthling is from another planet, want nothing to do with him.

Am all, "Do I look like a bitch?"

Escalator ends in what appears to be a gigantic room where furniture lives. Earthling who knows God walks away from me. It worked. Meanwhile, earthlings taking turns sitting on various couches, some red, some orange, some white. Inside earthlings are turning green. Thought: God is, like, in the furniture.

Am all, sitting on couch, "Should I complete the mission?"

No response.

Earthlings taking seats around me, turning green. Meanwhile, don't feel peace. Attached to the ceiling that's as high as the sky, lights burn all bright and shit.

Am all, "IKEA sucks."

[14.99]

Walking outside again. Sun melting parking lot.

Earthlings coming at me all gray, maybe full of fear. Two male earthlings behind me laughing. Looking through back of suit to see that inside they are filled with the same kind of laughter the policeling had—rattling shells. Continue walking, expanding inside the suit when I hear, "Nice pants, bow tie."

Turn around and say, "Thank you." At least they like my bow tie!

"Faggot," other says while, like, coughing.

"What?" I say, turning around.

They rush away, laughing still.

Now following other earthlings into a different building.

Inside, looking at myself in a mirror. Shirt so tight it's almost like I'm not wearing a shirt; "muscles," like, big. Turn this way, then other way. Wait . . . word "HOTTIE" written on buttocks portion, in white letters, on the black, stretchable pants took from female earthling's house. Colloquilator doesn't know these words. Question: What do they mean?

Return to IKEA. Find ATM. Remove all of its money.

Earthling male sees this, red tongues erupting in his stomach.

Go behind wall and place money in sphincter.

Return to car earthlings drove me in.

She and her little male not around. Go in the way I came—back door—and leave half of the money on pregnant female's seat.

[14.21]

Walking along the freeway, cars "honking" for some reason. Question: What is so "free" about the freeway? Follow-up question: Is it free of way?

"Hottie!" someone yells from car that flashes by.

Discovery: Can walk faster without shoes than with shoes.

Black air spits out tubes from cars and trucks. Thought: If earthlings suddenly, like, disappeared, Earth would be a planet of cars, revolving around the sun.

Darkness far away.

Don't know where to go for answers.

Thought: Have all the money I want. Can't seem to get what I want. Question: Does God exist?

Following "Sunset" sign, figuring that'll at least take me to the beach.

Am walking along street lined with palm trees and recognizing this is where the douche and me had driven in his Porsche. Question: Will he try to steal the suit again?

Earthlings waiting near a tall structure that says "In-N-Out" on it. Am all, approaching this short female whose insides are filled with brown boxes. Like the douche said, my senses are useless. Am all, "Does God exist?"

The woman turns orange inside. And then says, *"No hablo inglés."*

So I'm all, *"¿Existe Dios?"*

She's all, *"¿Me estas tornando el pels? ¡Por supuesto! ¿Que te pasa?"*

Am all, *"¿Te da respuestas?"*

She's all, *"Si."*

Am all, *"¿Por cierto—que esperas?"*

She's all, *"¡El autobus!"*

Am all, *"Gracias, Senorita."*

She's all, while coughing, *"¡Ducha!"*

Question: Did she just call me a douche?

[pause]

Am sitting on bus, thinking once again I've lost. It's weird, 'cause, like, every other earthling on the bus appears to be thinking the same thing.

167

Meanwhile, the sun has reached its highest point, melting the pavement. Earthlings around us trapped in cars. "Toxic," I say, staring out the window as another bus passes, its female earthlings all wearing the same clothing, mostly black, with black hats that have a white strip on them. Through the window I can see that they are all filled with what looks like green plants. Friendly.

I approach the driver. "How do I, like, get on that bus?"

"What bus?"

"That one."

"With the nuns?" He's all, looking down at the bare feet portion of my suit, "Man, do me a favor, don't stand up here while the god-damn bus is moving."

Return to the seat, where I'm looking out the window at the "nuns," contracting a little inside the suit.

One of the nuns—reminds me of the douche's wife—looks at me with what I used to think was fondness, the orange tongues rolling inside her chest.

She smiles. I give her the peace sign in response.

She laughs.

Am expanding, my molecules beginning to shake a little. Feels good. Now that Zoë hates me, maybe I could make love to this nun.

"I'm on the wrong bus!" I say to the nun, only this time the driver looks up at this mirror above him.

I turn away from the other bus, suddenly missing Zoë.

The earthlings on my bus are, like, neither homefree or wealthy. Most of them have bigger bodies than the wealthy earthlings. Weird that earthlings without money eat more. They wear clothing that looks like it was found—not bought. Then again, that's what I look like. Still don't get what's "united" about all these states. Suddenly find myself standing. Before the driver says anything, I reach into my sphincter.

Bus-riding earthlings are looking at me like I'm about to explode—this one earthling places his hands over his eyes, and fills with grayness. Meanwhile, I remove all the money I had put in there from the ATM and I start handing it, one by one, to these earthlings. Suddenly, they're all standing up and taking it, and so I just drop the money and walk up to the driver.

"Thank you, thank you!" I hear one of them say.

"That shit's counterfeit," another one says.

"Did that muhfucker just pull cash out his ass?"

[resume log: 13.00]

Mission aborted. Am leaving planet.

Thought: It has *not* been all good, motherfucker. Father, if I were talking to you, I'd—wait! Am receiving message.

[IN RESPONSE TO YOUR QUERY . . .
PLEASE REFRAIN FROM CONSUMING
PINKBERRY SUBSTANCE. THOUGH
UNCONFIRMED, WE HAVE REASON TO
SUSPECT ONE OF ITS INGREDIENTS COMES
FROM A NEIGHBORING PLANET, THUS
HINDERING THE MOTORY COMPLICATIONS
WITHIN YOUR SUIT]

[pause]

Okay, there's obviously, like, a delay on my questions for the scientists.

Meanwhile, the black ocean moans, spitting its white water onto the sand as I walk toward it.

"So what is the point of returning to my planet," I say, "if I've, like, lost here, wouldn't I just lose there?"

The water rushes at me, wanting to swallow me whole . . . only to retreat.

I have been on Earth for thirty-seven cycles or some shit, and I can't find earthling love. Even my suit gets to make love, just not with me in it. Am lying down on the sand so that the black water will cover the feet portion of my suit. I simply can't go on 'cause I don't know what is true or what is false on Earth.

The water doesn't swallow me, it only recedes. Before I know it, it's rushing at me again, only to recede. "Make a decision!" I say to the waves. Somewhere far out in the water is the craft. I do not engage it to encapsulate me. Eventually, for security reasons, it'll dissolve.

Maybe I should ask the water some questions.

"Should I defect and stay with Zoë?"

No response.

"Who's lying about the douche's mission? Him or Father or the committee or, like, all of them?"

No response.

Maybe the water only speaks Spanish. Of course, I can't speak Spanish without an earthling, like, addressing me in Spanish.

"Will I find earthling love with Zoë ?"

No response.

"Why does Earth suck so much?"

No response.

The moon seems to have disappeared somewhere, and so the water is rolling with more darkness than I've ever seen. I have grown so tired of being alone.

Without thinking, I find myself slipping out of the suit.

The ocean roars below me now as I ascend, the waves expanding and crashing over the suit, the arms and legs and head getting pulled into the water's angry stomach.

Little by little, beginning to expand, my molecules occupying space.

I let go . . . until I'm expanding at, like, such a rate that I'm hovering over a large portion of the ocean.

Uh-oh.

I am allowing molecules to expand. I am beginning to feel light. I am beginning to disappear. I am definitely evaporating. This is what Mother must have gone through. This black, scary fucking ocean . . . growing darker the farther I expand: white patches of water erupting in spots of endless black water, otherwise so black it appears all empty and shit like a gigantic hole in the earth. Like a . . . I am also expanding in the other direction, occupying space over the sector of Los Angles, below me roads filled with thousands and thousands of red and white electric eyes, all streaming alongside one another like the insides of a gigantic earthling . . . so much electric activity! Buildings burning with lights. Cars flashing with lights. Lights yellowing from the houses stuck into the hills. Blinking lights flickering on the aircrafts hovering over the city. Red lights flashing on top of buildings. I am spreading over the ocean and the city at the same time. I am occupying so much fucking space. I will occupy the entire planet I feel so light . . . I feel so made up of nothing and yet made of air. And I'm probably and totally evaporating and for some reason it's making me happy, which makes no fucking sense 'cause I am going to no longer exist. 'Cause I am disappearing . . . turning into everything molecule of air and water that is falling into the black ocean that spits it all back into the air, only to drop again, the water all carrying such a powerful force of gravity as I stretch over its black terrain. And I'm seeing lights on a . . . boat, and . . . in the other direction there are lights of an aircraft flying over Earth while I'm taking up space around that aircraft and breaking apart at such a rate I'm swallowing the aircraft with my molecules now; and it's rattling as it passes through me; and below the land no longer holds houses, only some cars driving on a black road along Earth, which is so gigantic as I am continuing to expand faster now that my molecules are stretching so far apart I don't know how my thoughts are holding together or where or what the fuck I am or if I laugh I will cause the wind to shift or if I cry I will cause rain and oh I have I simply become part of Earth 'cause . . . my thoughts are darkness my thoughts are light my thoughts are filling the ocean now, causing it to sway, causing it to groan and rush up onto the sand and then retreat and then I want to swallow an earthling and suck him into my angry stomach and it's just so fucking weird that I am the freeway hosting all these cars and that I am occupying earthlings emerging from restaurants with food in their bellies and that I am birds diving into the ocean and that my thoughts are animals running through the—

That's it! My *thoughts*!

I am beginning to disappear. Uh-oh. I am beginning to shrink.

Once again I am seeing the thousand electric eyes of the cars and the black ocean, and I'm shrinking and contracting and . . .

I'm seeing the beach again and then hovering over the area where I left the suit, only I don't see the suit. Wait, there's an arm, sticking out of the water. Quickly, I penetrate the water and enter the suit through its ear. Expand inside, taking control once again over its arms and legs and head; rattling with energy as I stand up, the waves crashing behind me. "My thoughts," I say, walking out of the water. The sound of my voice makes me laugh; the suit all shaking in that strange fashion. You know, if the mouth moves funny when I talk I don't give a fuck.

'Cause I found the answer!

"Clint!"

What the—a gigantic tongue of a wave slaps me from behind and tries to swallow me as I'm suddenly sliding so fast I don't know which way is up, sand all entering my mouth.

174

"Clint! You're drowning!!!"

"Zoë," I say, but she can't hear me.

Finally, I stand, only to get smashed by another wave until I'm spinning around in the black water again, laughing as I manage to stand while the ocean roars behind me, its tongues slapping me around, all reminding me that it can swallow me at any given moment. "Go head," I say. 'Cause I don't give a fuck! Everything makes me laugh. Everything on Earth is funny all of a sudden.

"My thoughts!" I say again into the water.

"Clint!" Zoë's saying with her hands over her mouth for some reason. "Swim!" she's saying.

"Swim!" I say as water fills the mouth portion. "Never learned that one."

"Clint, you can't swim!"

"Swim!"

"Yes!"

"Swim!"

"Can you?"

"No."

Zoë's running into the water and her jeans are all wet and she's pulling at the hand portion of my suit, and I'm wondering if the hand ripped off, would it make me laugh? Probably. Meanwhile, she's dragging me onto the dry sand, saying, "You're so heavy!"

The water has receded so that Zoë and I are sitting on a dry patch of sand. Then she's staring at me—her hair covering most of her face—when she, like, jumps onto me, and I fall back onto the sand.

"What's wrong with you, Clint?"

"My thoughts," I say, which sounds strange 'cause of all the water in my suit.

"Where the hell were you?"

"Everywhere at once."

"Are you okay? You have water in your mouth. Can you breathe? I totally followed you, by the way. I saw you walking and then I saw you, like, walking into the water and thought maybe you were going for a night swim and then, you, like, disappeared."

"My thoughts!"

"I totally thought you were—dead."

"I can't die, Zoë."

"Whatever, I'm just so glad you didn't—Jesus, Clint, what the hell are you wearing? Is that a bow tie?"

"Fuck! This thing is so douchey," I say, my suit rattling with laughter as I try to remove it.

Zoë laughs, and then reaches around my neck portion to remove it. "You're such a freak," she says, "you know that?" Then she presses her hands through my hairs and is all, "I was so worried about you, Clint. I mean, I'm still so mad—but I was worried."

Am expanding inside the suit so rapidly I'm worried I might explode, but I don't fucking care, 'cause I figured out the one answer to all my questions at once. I figured out the answers to, like, every earthling thing!

Zoë's all, "What's your fucking problem, anyway? Were you trying to, like, kill yourself?"

"Maybe."

"What's wrong with your voice?"

I put a hand to her face and say, "You are hurting, I can see that. I'm so sorry I, like, hurt you."

"You're such a loser for cheating on me!"

"Zoë, don't you get it!"

"Get what?"

"My thoughts."

"Uh . . . no."

"No one is a loser on Earth. And, like, no one's a winner, either. I figured it all out."

"Right," Zoë says, and then she gets off me and stands up, shoving hands into the pockets of her jeans. "It sounds like there's water in your mouth or something. You sure you're okay?"

Inside she is turning gray, orange bubbles erupting in her stomach area.

"Zoë," I say, looking into her eyes that, like, are covering these beautiful specs of light that I wish she could see. "I have to tell you something."

She's all, tears wetting her zits, "That you're, like, certifiably insane?"

"I'm not from this earth."

"You can say that again."

I say it again.

"Clinton, I'm only going to say this once. You've got a drug problem. But I can't help you. I was thinking all day today, like, if I ever saw you again, that you should take all of your daddy's money and put yourself into rehab. And I'm willing to help because I think you're sweet."

I stand up, and then with all my strength I contract and fill the finger portion of the suit, and then touch Zoë's neck, and all of her hairs are suddenly reaching into the air for space, and she's all, "Ouch! What the *hell* was that?" And she's holding her neck while I say, "How many of your earthling friends can do that?"

Zoë begins to walk all backward, then falls onto the sand, staring at me, these orange stars with gray hairs forms inside her. Shock. Ah! My senses. The douche was wrong. He was all wrong. Fuck the douche. Meanwhile, water is covering Zoë's body.

"Zoë! You okay?"

She stands up, and then walks away from me. "Just . . . leave me alone. Please don't mess with me anymore, okay? I don't know what you're doing, but it's really starting to freak me out." She's all walking away, her hair falling back to normal, and saying, "I'm *so* much smarter than you think."

"I think you're extremely smart."

"Whatever!"

I'm thinking of my thoughts again, and how, like, totally amazing I felt expanding and that—but inside that orange star with gray hairs melts into her silver puddle. "Look," I tell her, following her. But she starts running, and then I can't run. Fuck!

Eventually, she walks over to the "lifeguard" house and takes a seat on the "ramp." I finally catch up to her, and then I'm all, "Zoë, I have to tell you something."

"Whatever," she's saying, all grabbing her knees.

So I start explaining that I can see through her, that I can see her silver pond; that she's filled with sadness and fear right now. "It's just your opinion," she says, and I keep babbling. I babble everything, in fact. I babble that one, she doesn't need to be all afraid of anything; two, it's a major security risk but that I am from another planet; and three, I have this mission and shit. And she's all listening when she stands up and says, "What the—" and is reaching into my mouth, and then, like, starts pulling this long, green sea plant out from my mouth, with these green fingers attached to it. Finally, it all comes out. Zoë holds it up under the light of the moon. On the end of this sea plant is an old cellular phone.

"Ah," I say, all proud and shit, staring at the old phone that was inside my suit, "how many earthlings do you know can do *that*?"

"Holy shit," Zoë says, falling back against the lifeguard house, her eyes expanding so big I actually wonder if they could burst.

The black ocean scratches at our feet as we walk along the sand. Then Zoë's starts talking fast like: "This is so totally, like, overwhelming, Clint"—and then she looks up at me, and in her eyes I can see reflection of the moon—"I mean, I don't know if I'm crazy or want to be crazy, you know? Or if I want to believe in this stuff, 'cause I don't—I don't know what to think anymore, but . . . I think I believe you."

"Ah," I say, "good."

The waves are all scratching at the sand when she says, "Oh, my God, I have, like, so many questions for you. Oh, that sounded douchey, right?"

"I love douchey questions!"

"Okay, okay . . . like, do you have any special powers?"

"What the fuck is that supposed to mean?"

Zoë eats her fingernails for a while and then is all, "Like, do you have a special healing power or something?"

"Uh . . . if I do, I'm too much of a douche to know about it."

"Huh," Zoë says, these green lights flickering inside her head, "maybe we're the same way."

"Wait," I say, suddenly excited, "I can run on water!"

"No *way*!"

"Yeah." So I try to run. But I can't. Whatever. So I walk into the ocean and then try and, like, walk on the surface of the water. But I don't walk on it. I just walk into the water, and I'm standing there feeling stupid when a gigantic tongue slaps me down, and Zoë's all laughing.

"Sorry," I say, emerging from the water, my suit all wet.

"You're such a dork."

According to the colloquilator, a "dork" is a *stupid jerk*.

"Like," I say, "so be it."

Zoë is rattling with laughter.

Suddenly, the moon hides behind a cloud, and the ocean blackens, and Zoë turns all gray inside. Instead of all telling her not to fear I find myself thinking that's definitely why the earthlings are so crazy: 'Cause all the elements are constantly changing on Earth—the light, the darkness, waves, clouds, wind, and I'm sure a bunch of other stuff I don't know about. But instead of babbling this, I just say nothing. And what do you know! The moon returns, and a green bubble erupts inside Zoë's silver pond, and my molecules are quivering a little and I'm thinking that this is known as "peace."

I find myself explaining how I expanded, but she's never seen me outside of the suit. So I tell her how I expanded over possibly several states, or at least some sectors; over endless amounts of ocean, and it was just before I, like, evaporated, I realized my thoughts are what make my molecules. And that my molecules make my thoughts. *"That's* my answer, Zoë! I'm, like, a mist of thoughts. It's so fucking simple. If I change my thoughts, you know, I change me."

"I don't know," Zoë says, shoving her hands in her pockets as she walks, "I mean, it kind of makes sense. But it's also, like, way abstract."

"What the fuck is that supposed to mean?"

"Don't raise your voice at me!"

"Wait, I just told you about the way I found all my answers, and you were all, like . . . who cares?"

"First off, I didn't, like, say who cares. Second off, if you have some sort of like, epiphany, then that's yours. And no one can take that away from you. I'm so sorry, I didn't mean to, like, make light of it."

"Actually," I find myself saying, "you're right."

"I am always right," Zoë says through a smile.

"Maybe."

Zoë hits me in the chest portion. And together we start to laugh, and then she's saying it makes total, like, sense that I laugh like a weirdo 'cause I'm from "outer space," and I'm all expanding inside the suit as I say, "Zoë! I just thought of something else."

"What?"

"Come back to my planet with me."

"Oh my God," Zoë says, and then she starts hopping from one leg to another, "oh my—can we do that?"

"Yes!"

"Oh my God, yes, Clinton! Yes! Please, take me back!"

She jumps up on my suit and I'm all, trying to hold her when we crash onto the sand. "Clinton," she's saying, kissing my face portion. I kiss her back, this time inserting my tongue into her mouth. "Ouch," she says.

"What's wrong?"

"So that's why you're always shocking me."

"Sorry."

"It's okay."

Zoë sits on my chest portion now. "No, isn't there a way you can, like, make it less?" She leans down, and again we kiss, this time I contract into the middle of the suit, and she says, "Better."

"Let's make love!"

Inside Zoë turns to orange, and then she's staring off at the waves and saying, "I'm . . . a virgin."

According to the colloquilator, "virgin" is *the mother of Christ*.

"Wait," I say, "you had a child?"

"What? No!"

"You sure?"

"Gosh, you really don't know anything." Zoë wipes her nose. "A virgin is a girl who, like, hasn't had sex yet."

"Oh. That sucks."

"It doesn't suck, Clint."

"Wait, I'm, like, a male virgin then!"

Suddenly a brown wall begins to rise out from Zoë's pond and she's all, "You sure about that?"

"Yes. Let's make love!"

Something is wrong with her. I think it's rage or . . . hostility? Doesn't make sense. She's all, "I guess I'm worried that you're, you know—your dick would hurt me, it's too big."

"Not for Karen, it wasn't."

"That the slut in our bed you were with?"

I explain who Karen is, and how the douche had stolen my suit and had sex with her while he had me captive.

"Wait," Zoë says, and then rolls off of me, all silver inside. "That's, like, the worst excuse ever. And it's totally sleazy."

"I'm not lying, Zoë."

"I want to believe you, Clinton. I do. But you were with that slut."

"I was only in the bed with her for, like, three hours, Zoë."

"Ew!"

She's all getting up and walking away when I say, "Wait, no—maybe minutes. I don't know what an hour is, Zoë."

Zoë stops and turns around, and her eyes flicker and shit under the light of the moon, and I'm all, "You are beautiful, Zoë."

She's all, "Thanks."

I'm all, "I'm sorry for hurting you."

"I appreciate that."

"I was confused."

"Well," she says, looking down at the feet portion of my suit, "I guess you are, like, an alien and stuff."

"Totally."

Zoë grabs me, presses her breasts against the suit. I shrink to the chest portion to meet her molecule, and then begin to rattle. Then I find myself reaching down with the hands to squeeze her buttocks.

"You have nice buttocks," I tell her.

She laughs, and her body shakes. "Oh yeah, you like my ass?"

I squeeze it harder now, each of its cushions a round planet I'd like to explore. Ass, I think, and then the penis portion grows. Zoë doesn't move, though, she leans up against me and breathes into my chest. And I'm wondering if maybe we can make earthling love when Zoë's all, talking into the neck portion of my suit, "It's just going to take a little while before, like, I can trust you again, Clinton."

[resume log: 11.01]

Female earthling named Zoë will be returning with me. Please send instructional on how to fit her into the craft. Lates.

[10.77]

Zoë yelling at earthlings who've taken over our house. One by one, they leave.

Thought: Earthlings don't like to be yelled at.

Kip is nowhere to be seen. Searched everywhere: behind the couch, in the bathtub, in the backyard. Meanwhile, beer cans and bottles lying all over carpet. Kitchen so, like, cluttered with garbage it's difficult to find the sink. Am all, "What happened?"

"I stopped sleeping here," Zoë says, blue and orange bubbles intersecting inside her, "so I guess this is Kip's mess. I'm so sorry, Clint."

"Are you full of shame?"

"You paid for all this."

"It's the bank's money."

"Yeah but you did a perfectly nice thing and Kip just, like, peed all over it. He's like my dad, he has no appreciation for good things." Zoë starts eating her fingernails. "For sure."

"Kip is just afraid."

"I guess."

"All earthlings are afraid."

"You must think that we—like, us humans are total losers."

"Don't use that word, Zoë."

"Whatever—it's just a word."

I sit down on a chair in the kitchen, watching Zoë as she places stuff in the sink, her sandy hair reaching halfway down her back. "That's what I don't like about Earth."

"What?"

"That it's all separated into winners and losers. Why can't there just be, like, earthlings?"

Water is flowing now as Zoë pours an orange liquid into the sink. "I guess we love to, like, put people into categories."

"Maybe that's why little earthlings are always full of fear, 'cause they're losers until some douche shows up and is all, 'You're a winner!'"

"Huh." Zoë removes her hands from the bubbles, which, like, cling to her skin. "But you call people douche all the time—isn't that, like, calling someone a loser?"

I'm all, "Huh."

I'm thinking she's, like, smarter than me. So I try to sound all smart and shit. "Wait. No. A douche is, like, not born a douche. He, like, becomes one at some point. A loser is born a loser, you know, if he lives in a poor sector. Make sense?"

"Kind of . . ."

Am thinking I should sound even smarter now. So I'm all, "Anyway—it's your *thoughts* that can change everything, Zoë."

"Change what? The Earth is melting."

I go to the window and look outside. A palm tree stands still under a road lamp. "The Earth is melting?"

"Duh. Global warming."

She's putting glass bottles into this big black bag. Her gray puddle is leaking out of her eyes now, and I'm sensing I shouldn't talk about this kind of stuff right now. So I'm all, trying to make her laugh, "You know a female earthling told me, like, in Spanish that I'm a douche."

"Really?" Zoë says, but she doesn't laugh. And now I'm suddenly shrinking, kind of feeling sad for her; and remembering the craft will dissolve soon if I don't return to it. And then I'm all thinking of the douche, and I'm watching Zoë spray a green substance all over the kitchen when it hits me—I will ask Zoë to help me complete the mission. "Zoë," I say, "I have a mission."

"Okay."

"You can help me complete it. Then we can return to my planet."

"Totally," she says, her entire body filling with gray liquid, "but can we just clean first? You know, then start your mission thingy. I just hate to leave the place like this."

[pause]

"What's your planet like?" Zoë wants to know, driving what I think is totally too close to the car in front of us. We took Kip's car. Meanwhile, I'm wearing Kip's clothes, 'cause Zoë thought I looked douchey in my hottie pants.

"Do you know how to drive?"

"Oh what, they got cars on your planet?"

"No, but I don't think you're supposed to drive this close to—"

"I told you, Clint, I don't have my license yet, all right? This dumbass car is the size of a cruise ship. Kip bought this car 'cause it's the same year as him, back when, cars were, like"—Zoë starts talking Kip—"badass *motherfuckers*, man."

Meanwhile, the car appears to be swaying in one direction and, like, driving in another. Zoë is so full of fear her skin is almost turning gray. She's all moving her hands now and doing everything but touching the wheel: "I don't even know where the windshield wiper cleaner thingy is."

"Who's that doucheling on the—"

"Hood?"

There's a gigantic picture of a friendly-looking earthling with long hair on the hood.

"Jerry Garcia."

"Wait, he's from the Deathly Grateful."

"Something like that."

"I don't know why they're so grateful."

"You're cute for an alien, you know that. For sure."

"Zoë," I say all seriously and shit, trying to make her laugh so that her puddle inside doesn't fill up with fear as she's driving, "according to an instructional, I'm meant to eat baby earthlings for strength. Can you find me one?"

"Are you *fucking* serious?"

The sun is heating the "freeway" as all the cars have stopped. I'm wondering how there are so many cars and so, like, little road when Zoë's all, "What's life like on your planet?"

Written into the big hill it says "HOLLYWOOD" in white letters. For some reason I don't feel like answering Zoë about my planet; in fact, I'm all trying to imagine the douche's first day on Earth. Meanwhile, Zoë's all, "Earth to Clinton."

"My planet," I tell her, "is, like, the opposite of Earth in almost— every way."

"What, like, you don't have Starbucks?"

According to the colloquilator, Starbucks is *expensive.*

"For real," Zoë says, "you mean it's not, like, totally assed-out and polluted?"

"Wait, the whole Earth is polluted?"

"Definitely all the cities. But I think the ocean is too from all the crap. Don't get me wrong, it's a beautiful planet, it's just . . . 'cause of all the pollution over the last hundred years or whatever, it's melting. It has to do with carbon monoxide. I mean, sometimes I think we're going to make it better, you know? And sometimes I, like, totally think we're screwed." Zoë starts touching one of her zits with a finger. "So what's your planet like, dude?"

"I don't know . . . we don't have roads or buildings."

"So what do you have?"

"Everything's made of what you would call, like, electrical energy. Does that make sense?"

"Kind of."

For some reason, I don't feel like explaining all of it to her. "I miss it," I find myself saying, which is the truth.

"Okay. Like, what do you miss about it?"

"I don't know—it's just such a simple place."

She places her hand on the hand portion of my suit, and together, like that, with our molecules joined, we roar past the palm trees and up the hill toward Mulholland Drive.

[resume log: 08.77]

Kip's car all rattling as we stop in front of a wooded section. Sun dropping, but still melting trees and roads. Zoë's forehead is wet with sweat. She's all wiping it when I say, "So remember the plan. I came here to, like, beg the douche to put me into a film. And I don't care that he, you know, tried to steal the suit."

"Right—wait, do you really think if you guys, like, made up, you could act?"

"No, I don't believe anything he says. Besides, acting is douchey."

"Not all actors are douches."

"They're not?"

"Some actors are total artists. For sure."

"I don't know how to act, Zoë."

"Clinton, you should have more confidence. You'd make a terrific actor."

"Really?"

"Totally. And you could, like, explore a different side of yourself, you know?"

"Like, my sphincter?"

Zoë rattles with laughter, and then fills with orange liquid. Am feeling suddenly fearfree and shit, and fucking loving it. "Don't be afraid, Zoë," I say, expanding inside, "it's your *thoughts* that make you afraid."

"Whatever."

"Whatever?"

We must remain strong, I want to tell her, but am thinking she just needs to, like, figure this out on her own. Wanting to tell her that part now. But can't say that, 'cause saying it, like, weakens it or something—confusing.

Red car screams past us, its driver wearing sunglasses.

"I don't have a good feeling about this," Zoë says, squeezing hand portion so hard on my suit. Don't know why, but find myself kissing her. She makes strange sound that comes up from her chest. "Mmm."

Penis stiffens. Ignoring it.

I walk into the wooden section, Zoë following me. I reach into the sphincter, searching for apprehension device.

"Uh," Zoë says, "what are you doing?"

"This is part of my mission."

Zoë laughs.

"What's so funny?"

"Nothing."

"I'm searching for apprehension device, Zoë."

"Right."

"Fuck!"

"What's wrong?"

"I can't find it."

"Right."

"Can you, like, help me? It must have gotten moved somehow when I had money up there."

"Okay," Zoë says. Then she's all eating her fingernails. "Wait, you had, like, money up your butt?"

"Zoë, we don't have much *time*."

"Don't yell at me, Clinton."

"I'm not yelling!"

"Yes you are."

"You're making me yell!"

"Oh yeah, that's mature!"

We're all staring at each other. This brown wall erupts from within Zoë's stomach and begins to, like, rise. Not sure what it is. Anger? No. Hostility, maybe? According to colloquilator, "hostility" is *opposition to something*.

"You're hostility."

"Excuse me?" Zoë says, and then she's all looking down at the dirt. "Look, let's just . . . Tell me what you need, Clinton."

"I need for you to reach into the sphincter of my earthling suit and help me find this device."

"No," Zoë says all loud like, "freaking way!"

"Zoë, are you going to help me complete the mission or not?"

"Yes, but . . ."

"But what?"

"Clinton Eastwood, I do *not* want to go up your butt!"

"It's not real, Zoë. You know? This suit. It's not real."

Zoë going all silent; green bubbles erupting inside her silver pond. Then green bubble bursts into black pointy things that fill her body.

"Relax your thoughts," I say.

"Enough about my thoughts!"

"Fine. Be that way."

"Okay, I will."

"Whatever."

"So you, like, want me to go"—she gets all quiet—"up your *ass* to get some apprehensive thingy?"

"*Apprehension* device. Yes."

"I'm sorry. I won't do it."

"You know," I find myself saying, like, without realizing it, "you're . . . I don't know the word."

"What a surprise."

"Females are nuts. Kip was right."

"Oh, and this coming from a freakin' alien?"

"That is so not fair, Zoë."

"Clinton, don't you *ever* tell me what's fair!"

"What the fuck is that supposed to mean?"

"You know, you can't just keep using that. One of these days it's going to come back and haunt you."

"What the fuck is that supposed to mean?"

"Stop it," she says, covering her ears.

"What the fuck is that supposed to mean?"

"*STOP* it!!!"

"I'm sorry," I find myself saying while a gigantic truck roars past.

Zoë hugs me, and then speaks into my neck portion, "You know what that was?"

"A truck?"

"No, silly. Our first fight."

Penis stiffens. Zoë continues to press herself against me, like she's not afraid of it.

I kiss her. Her tongue gets inserted into my mouth. I grab her butt.

Crashing to the floor of woods now.

Zoë sitting on my stomach portion, leaning down to kiss me.

Reaching up to grab her breasts under her shirt; her nipples all hard. Dick growing inside jeans. Zoë laughs, then stops laughing. Then rubs hand over jeans. Molecules beginning to vibrate. Uh-oh. Expanding inside. Feeling . . .

Zoë sitting on me, rubbing against dick portion that wants to escape from its hiding place in jeans.

Suit beginning to vibrate. Molecules rattling inside.

Entire suit now beginning to shake. Zoë says, her breathing all strange, "Oh-oh-oh my-my-my God-duh-duh-duh."

Molecules growing so big inside it's like I can name them if I wanted. Wait . . . am beginning to blink inside.

Zoë's all looking up at the sky, sounding like she's having trouble breathing. Inside this, like, yellow flower grows out from within her, and she's all, "Oh!"

And then the flower shrinks, and she's, like, losing her breath.

Molecules have gone numb. Have lost feeling. Have begun expanding at such a rate that I . . . disappear.

Where am I?

"Wow," Zoë says, looking down at me.

[pause]

Not really sure if we made love, but don't want to ask for some reason. We were all hugging afterward when I reminded Zoë of the device. I think it wasn't until she finally extracted it from the sphincter that she fully realized I am, like, not from Earth. Instead of being all cool about this, though, she's sad.

"You have to be strong," I tell her as we're all walking along the road toward the douche's house now.

"I know," she says, moving hair from her eyes. Then she says, "You know it's very, like . . . cute."

"What?"

"This device thingy," Zoë says, holding it. "Gosh, it's like a cheese ball."

She's laughing, tears coming out of her eyes. Laughing and crying. Earthlings are amazing beings! Am all, "What, you don't have one of those in your sphincter?"

"Just you—*pain* in my ass."

A black car rushes past; and suddenly we both get all serious and shit.

"I'm worried," she says, grabbing my hand portion. I feel her molecules rattling next to mine and am all, "What is worry, anyway?"

"I don't know." Zoë laughs.

"Me neither."

We see the translucent wall. We're getting closer. "Remember our plan," I say.

"Right . . . what's the plan again?"

"Focus, Zoë!"

"Don't yell at me, Clinton!"

"I didn't yell."

"Tell me again, I mean, I know the plan, but—"

"Okay. I'm going to, like, *pretend* I'm here to beg the douche to put me in a film."

"Right. And you're going to, like, *pretend* not to care that he tried to steal your suit?"

"Totally. This way I can apprehend him when he's not suspecting."

Zoë looks down at the pavement and then is all, "He's not going to believe you."

"Yes he will."

"You sure?"

"Yes! Fuck fear. Fuck him. Fuck everything."

Pink tongues erupt inside her, and she's all, "Wow, Clinton, that's kind of hot to hear you talk like that."

I kiss Zoë, and then grab her hand portion, and we're crossing the road. Meanwhile, I'm trying to sense if he's in the house or not when Zoë's all, "What if, like, he steals the suit again and tries to kill me?"

"Are you serious?"

"Look, I've never been on one of these mission thingies, Clint— so don't expect me to be all . . . full of courage and stuff."

"Don't let your thoughts, like, control you. It's that simple."

"Okay, but—the plan totally sucks."

"Stay here then. I'll do it myself!"

"Don't talk to me like that."

"I'm sorry, Zoë, it's just . . . just trust me, it's going to be okay."

Zoë's looking at me as I walk back and forth now, and then it hits me. "Okay, maybe you're right, the plan isn't that great. So what if, like, along with me wanting to be in the film, *you* also want it—like, you want a big house with a view and shit?"

"That's good! And 'cause all *you* care about is sex, I convince you."

"Yes!"

Zoë smiles, and then walks up to me and we kiss, my molecules flapping.

"I think we make a good team, Clinton, you know that?"

The penis portion is starting to move. I ignore it.

"Wait," I find myself saying, "you think all I care about is sex?"

[resume log: 07.99]

Pressing button that says "call" next to it. Female saying through device, "Jack?"

"It's the wife," I say to Zoë, "Karen."

"Yes?"

"Shh!" Zoë says.

"I see you brought a friend?"

"Uh," I say, wondering if she's got some special powers of sight, "yes."

Zoë hits me in the back portion for some reason, and then points to an electric eye. Ah! Camera. "Jack?" the wife says. "I thought you moved back to Nebraska."

"I did?"

"I'm Zoë," Zoë says, giving me this weird look.

I'm all, suddenly remembering what the douche had told me, "I grew up with a motheraholic."

"Douche," Zoë whispers to me.

"Don't call me a douche!"

"*Douche!*"

"Stop that!"

"Shh."

Meanwhile, the big door begins to rattle and then slowly rolls open, revealing the two gigantic glass boxes that sit next to each other: The douche's home.

"Oh," Zoë says as we're walking up the driveway, "my God!"

Standing outside douche's house. Apprehension device in pocket of jeans. Prepared to apprehend. Zoë filled with green tongues. "You think we could live like this, Clint? I mean, you know, if we didn't go to your planet?"

Thought: Sensing he's not here. Question: Has he come up with a way of, like, blocking me from sensing him?

"Then again," she's saying, "I doubt him or his wife is, like, happy, you know, I mean, she can't have his babies, right?"

Thought: Suit had sex with Karen. Question: Is she going to want more?

"What're you thinking about?" Zoë says, that brown wall rising inside her.

"Nothing, why?"

"Did you have sex with this woman, Clint?"

"Zoë, I told you. No."

"I believe you."

"The suit did."

"Right." Then Zoë's all biting on her fingernails and saying, "Ew!"

"What?"

"Just the thought of it, it's sleazy."

Thought: This earthling female is always trying to prove me wrong.

Walking around gigantic palm tree that's standing in grass. Zoë squeezes hand portion. Her energy—relaxing me.

"You sure we can't get arrested or something, Clint? I mean, he's, like, famous."

About to say no when front door opens.

Karen appears, her red hair all resting on top of her head; wearing all white, baggy clothing. Suddenly, inside her a black wall begins to rise.

"Who's this again?" Karen says.

"Hi," Zoë says, walking up the steps, "I'm Zoë."

"Karen," the wife says, smiling, inside a red bar growing on top of her wall.

"Was he expecting you?"

Am all, "No."

Zoë's all, "Yes."

Am all, "Maybe."

"Right," Karen says, "well, he's just having a lunch meeting, but come on in."

[pause]

Gigantic windows reveal the entire earth, it seems, clouds bumping each other over so many houses and roads and trees it's like we're sitting in an aircraft that's hovering over the entire sector of Los Angeles.

Meanwhile, sunlight spills through the glass walls, splashing the red rug, much of the furniture, and Zoë, who's all, turning to red tongues inside. "This view is unfuckingbelievable! Oh my God, that pool is—wow."

"Oh, it's all right," Karen says, rubbing her hair.

"Really?" The tongues flap so fast inside Zoë it's like she's filled with a light. "You mean you don't like it?"

"Kidding. It's fabulous, right? We had that done just last fall. It's called an infinity pool."

"Infinity," Zoë says, "for sure."

I give Zoë a look, like to say, "Yeah—like you know what an infinity pool is." And she's all, returning a look, like to say, "At least I can defecate."

"Take a seat," Karen says, rattling with strange laughter as she exits the room, "just make sure to return it."

Then Karen's all talking to us from the kitchen so that we can't see her. "Can I ask you guys something?"

"Sure," Zoë says.

"You guys are of the teen demographic, right?"

"I guess," Zoë says, giving me a look, like to say, "Duh."

"It's just that—well, my husband thinks he's too recognizable to play any dramatic roles—at least that's what some of the indie producers are telling him. Which is just, you know, a load of shit. But—I mean, do you guys think that?"

"Totally," Zoë says.

I cover her mouth, and she, like, breaks free.

"What the hell?" she whispers. "Tell her no," I whisper back.

"I mean, then again," Zoë says to Karen, "if I, like, really had to think about it, I'd totally pay to see him in a dramatic movie. For sure."

"That's what I thought," Karen says from the other room, "but you know actors. *So* insecure."

"Idiot."

"Don't you *dare* call me that."

"Duh, that's why he wants my suit. To, like, be a young actor again."

"Oh," she says, "sorry."

"It's okay."

The furniture, like the douche, appears too perfect for this earth—plastic, with the material like Kip's jacket. "Leather," I say to Zoë, trying to, like, talk about something else in case Karen walks in.

"Shh."

"Wait—what I do wrong? I thought *you* just, like, did something wrong."

"Drinks?" Karen shouts from the kitchen.

"Beer," Zoë says, and smiles at me.

"Why not?" Karen shouts back. "Minors got to live too, right?"

"*Hell's* yeah," Zoë says, and then, to me, she's all, in a lower voice, "*Love* her, I mean . . . maybe."

I'm all, "You think she's, like, acting weird?"

"Duh," Zoë whispers, "she slept with your . . ."

"Suit?"

"Yes. And she feels threatened that, like, you're here with me."

I think about this and am all, "You're very smart."

"It took you this long to figure that out," Zoë says, getting up. I'm watching her walking around the room examining photos and shit. "Oh, here's totally Jack Nicholson!" she says. "And is that Elizabeth freaking Taylor? She looks, like, old. My mom used to *worship* her."

My molecules begin to rattle. Something's happening.

"Zoë," I whisper.

Meanwhile, Karen walks in with a "tray" on which she's placed beer bottles. "No more than one," she says, "I don't feel like getting arrested today . . . *again*. Oh, I'm just kidding."

"Ha!" Zoë laughs. As she's lowering the tray to the table, Karen stares at me; behind her eyes I see this red, blinking light.

"Say thanks, Clinton."

"Oh," Karen says, the red light blinking faster now, "you call him Clinton?"

I'm all vibrating on the couch, "Thanks."

"You're welcome, Clinton," Karen says, reaching into her pocket to retrieve a phone. "Hey," she says, talking into the phone as she leaves the room.

"Something's happening," I tell Zoë, "he's here."

Zoë begins to walk back and forth in front of the wall of windows. "You sure you know what you're doing?"

"No."

"Are you serious?"

Red bubbles are erupting inside her silver pond when I'm all, "But that's just it—you know? I don't think I can ever know. It just *feels* right."

Zoë's nodding, staring out the window. Meanwhile, my molecules are beginning to rattle so much the arms of the suit are rising upward. "He's definitely here," I say.

"Clinton," Zoë whispers, joining me on the couch, "that's kind of hot that you sensed him—for sure." She kisses my cheek, and then says, "Ouch!"

"Shh."

"Everything okay?" Karen shouts from another room.

"Uh," Zoë says, "totally!"

A door opens. Zoë looks at me, squeezing the sides of her chair, her little pond bubbling over. Karen shouts from some room, "Hon, is that you?"

"Yes, babe."

"Your friend is here," she shouts. "You know—the one who looks like a young Clint Eastwood?"

[resume log: 7.10]

The douche stands in front of the window, staring at us. His hair is shorter, all black and shiny; he changed its color. Meanwhile, his being inside his suit has formed into a blue V of molecules. Uh-oh. It means he's happy I'm here. But he's lying. He has to be lying!

"So," he says in this deep, strange, almost electric voice, "we meet *again*?"

"Hi," Zoë says.

"Oh. This is Zoë."

"Nice to see you," the douche says, his teeth sparkling as he smiles.

Thought: Will have to control thoughts so as, like, to act like I'm not here to apprehend him. Wait—did he just sense that last thought? Fuck!

Calming my molecules, am all, "I want to be in a film."

"Totally," Zoë says, "I think he should."

"I guess we're skipping the preambles," the douche says, and smiles. "All business, eh, Clint?"

"You have, like, an amazing house," Zoë says.

"Like," the douche says, "thanks."

"I know," Zoë says. "I say 'like' a *lot*."

"Please," the douche says, "don't sweat it. It's cute."

Zoë's face has turned red; inside her white tongues flap.

"Zoë, so you think Clint here would make a good actor?"

"For sure."

"For sure?"

"That means yes."

"I know what it means, Clint."

"I mean," Zoë says, "he's, like, innocent—so he could use that, right?"

Am beginning to shrink a little. Fuck. Must focus. "Yeah," I say, "like, what she said."

"Well, maybe we can test him out and see. Zoë, what're you drinking?"

"Beer," Zoë says, "is fine."

The douche leaves the room, and then says, "Clint, can you come in here, please?"

Exploding inside the suit, occupying each part, the energy making me stand. "You okay?" Zoë whispers. Then she's all, "He's, like, totally strange up close. I can see the, you know—he looks so fake. I mean, like you."

"Thanks."

"Clint," she says, finishing the beer Karen had brought, "he doesn't seem all that, you know, bad."

"Every word out of his mouth is a lie, Zoë."

"How do you know?"

"I just do," I lie.

Truth is, I completely *feel* it's the truth. So maybe it's not a lie. Am about to meet the douche in the other room when Zoë's all, "Clint." She's smiling now as she sits on the couch. And I can't help but smile a little, and then, in a loud whisper she's all, "You're the sexiest alien I know. Kick his ass!"

Thinking about telling her that he doesn't really have an ass— but I decide against it. Meanwhile, I'm expanding now, staring at hair that could totally be a mixture of sand and soil and the beautiful red spots on her face, and it's like she was born out of the ocean. And so I'm all, "You're a fish."

"Uh," she says, "I guess that's a compliment."

[pause]

Like he's waiting for me, the douche sits at the gigantic black table on which a pile of lemons has been set. He's all using a gigantic knife to cut open a lemon. "So. How you've been, man?"

"I want to be in a film," I say, trying with all my strength to believe this.

"Sure. I can intro*douche* you to some casting directors. We'll get you tested."

"Introdouche," I say, relaxing my molecules, "that's really funny."

"It's your invention, my man."

I laugh all loud and shit and then say, "Yeah. Cool."

He stands up from his seat, picks up three lemons, and starts throwing them into the air, catching and throwing each one so fast it looks like the lemons are traveling on their own. I'm, like, totally impressed, but I won't tell him that.

Meanwhile, he puts the lemons back in a pile and then says, his teeth all sparkling as he smiles, "Douche."

"You're the douche," I say, and then I'm laughing a little now as I reach into my pocket.

And he's laughing a little now.

Suddenly, we both stop laughing.

And the douche just stares at me, his being expanding inside.

So, y'know, I throw the apprehension device at him.

It bounces off of his leg and then falls to the floor.

Meanwhile, he's still standing there, his being still trapped inside his suit.

Fuck!

"What the," he says, looking down at the apprehension device, "hell is that?"

Must focus.

"Cheese ball," I lie. "Zoë gave it to me, but you know . . . I don't— eat?"

I'm leaning down to retrieve it when the douche's shoe smashes my face portion so that I'm, like, totally standing up now. Before I get a chance to calm my molecules the douche drives a fist into the stomach portion of my suit.

And I'm leaning against the wall, my being rattling inside. Then he's digging his finger into nose portion of my suit. "Don't," I say.

"Don't what?"

I'm trying with all my strength to reach up into his face and dig into his stupid nose. At the same time, I'm moving my head and turning around and around so that he can't get into my suit and before I know it we're all standing on other sides of the room, staring at each other. Except, something's totally different about his face. Then it hits me: He's missing his nose.

'Cause I'm holding it.

Where it used to be is this, like, blue strip. I must have unlocked it from his face or some shit.

"Clint," he says in a very serious voice, "give it back."

I slip the nose into my pocket and say, "You're coming back with me."

"Hand it over. Don't be stupid."

"Hon!" Karen says again from upstairs, and then quickly the douche runs out of the room and then he's suddenly standing in the kitchen again.

"You stole my suit," I say, "'cause you were going to act in films you could never act in yourself."

"You're an idiot."

"No I'm not!"

"I just used it to have"—he's all lowering his voice—"sex with Karen."

"That's a lie."

That V inside him is shrinking, turning red, his molecules all tiny now. "Believe me, she truly enjoyed it. You should be proud of your suit."

"That's stupid. Wait, she really enjoyed it?"

"Trust me, it's always been a fantasy of hers to have sex with a younger guy. I wanted to make it happen for her. That's it, man. The beauty is, she thinks she cheated on me, but I know. Trust me, I was going to return it after."

"You were acting in it. I saw you."

"Oh, I was just going over some lines—just playing around. No big deal."

"You were going to evaporate me."

"Gosh, you must think I'm a lunatic."

According to the colloquilator, a . . . uh-oh; his molecules are forming into one red cube. "You sure," he's saying, walking toward me, "you're not just an errand boy?"

"Don't call me that."

"Sent by grocery clerks!"

He moves against my suit in a way that I'm suddenly lying on the floor. He reaches down, pressing his fingers so hard into my neck portion that I can't move, and then he unlocks my head from my suit.

"Give it back," I say, lying all headless and shit on the floor.

Each of his molecules has turned black, except this one in the center that's silver . . . and slowly turning red. "You have *no* idea what you're getting yourself into, my friend."

"You, like, betrayed me."

"Welcome to the earth, Mr. Eastwood," he says, throwing the head into the air and catching it, "get used to it."

"Give it back."

"Give me back the nose, and you get this back."

"No."

"Fine." He walks out of the room with my head. "Zoë," I hear him say, "catch."

He comes back in. And then the douche and me are staring at each other, like we're waiting for . . .

"AAAAAAaaaaaaahhh!"

I rush into the room to get my head, and then I'm all, standing there headless and shit, realizing this is probably difficult for her. So I'm all, "Zoë, don't be afraid."

Inside, she's turned into these swelling, gray waves. She climbs back onto the chair, my head lying on the floor. "Why don't," the douche says, all noseless, sliding open the gigantic glass door, "you and your companion here leave. All will be forgiven. How's that sound, Zoë?"

"Uh," Zoë says.

Karen is all yelling from upstairs, "What's going on, hon? Did someone scream?"

"We're just acting out a scene, sweetheart!"

The douche then grabs my head portion and throws it through the open glass door.

And I'm all expanding inside the suit when I hear a splash.

"Zoë," I say, "get my head. Then wait for me outside. Please." Zoë's nodding at me, afraid to speak, it seems. "Be strong, Zoë. You can do it!"

"How are you speaking?" she says.

"Colloquilator," I say.

She runs out of the room. And I'm all, "She's no longer in love."

"Sorry to hear that," the douche says, walking toward me.

"I was talking about your wife."

"Please," he says in our language, "I told you. Your senses—they're off."

"She had sex with my suit. She wants *me*."

"Who do you think was in that suit, my friend?"

Meanwhile, that knife erupts inside him again.

"Ah," I say, "you're full of envy."

"So," he says, "you told Zoë about who you are, eh?"

"What do you care?"

"Does she know about me?"

"Yes."

"You know what I'm going to do for you, Copper? I'm going to stuff you into a ring box. You know what a ring box is? Of course you don't. Then I'm going to glue it shut. Wrap it in inches of duct tape. And then FedEx the fucker to NASA. How's that sound?"

Real slow like, he's chasing me around the table.

I'm walking backward, trying to, like, distract him now—trying to get him all angry. "No one," I say, "wants to see you in film. You've made stupid busterblocks."

"Idiot." He laughs. "You can't even speak."

Suddenly, his suit falls to the carpet, like it's dead.

Uh-oh.

He's hovering over me now: "Did you ever think you could actually accomplish this mission, errand boy?"

[resume log: 6.92]
Wooden ceilings so high it seems a spaceship can fit in here. Meanwhile, his molecules have taken over entire room, a cloud of tiny blue and red balls all slowly bouncing off one another.

He's much stronger than I'd imagined, much bigger than me. A brown dog walks out from the kitchen and begins to sniff the head portion of that face the youthful earthlings worship.

Dog's tail wiggles back and forth.

Meanwhile, I walk into the kitchen and sit down at the table suddenly, pretending I haven't all slipped out the earthling suit.

"I can see," he says, having followed me into the room, "that you're out of the suit."

Fuck! Something white flashing. He's gone into the electrical wiring. Thought: Don't know how to do that.

Lights in the house begin to blink. Question: Is he gaining strength? Am shrinking a little. Must . . . be strong. Controlling my thoughts . . . fuck!

Contracting to the size of an earthling hair. Am entering slits in wall that plugs go into. Being sucked into these wires and it isn't long before everything turns white. . . .

Something grabbing a hold of me. Can't see. Am being shocked. Can't . . . move.

Being pulled through wires.

Losing . . . vision. He's getting to me.

"Stop!" I say in our language. I can't see him. Molecules burning.

I break free. Now floating in center of a room that has a gigantic TV. Molecules, have, like, disappeared. Need to rest.

Can't rest. Need to rest. Uh-oh.

The apprehension device.

Quickly, I drift into kitchen and retrieve it from the jeans pocket of my suit. Karen walks in, sees the douche's body, and then begins to do what I think is called "scream." It turns to a moan as gray snakes tangle up inside her. "Oh," she says, "my God. What happened to your . . . nose?"

I'm watching her and thinking she looks much prettier with her face all wet from tears for some reason. Meanwhile, the gray snakes inside her are expanding and turning black. Fuck it. I slip into her body so as to distract her.

"What the—" she says.

Her body warm; moist. Beginning to experience what must be . . . oh no! Am feeling love with the douche's wife. Thought: Zoë will get mad.

Am sensing the douche entering the room. He enters his own suit, and then is all, "Karen, it's okay, honey, it's okay. Relax—I can explain everything."

"Something's inside me," Karen says, her voice all shaking, "I think I'm dying."

Contracting into a ball, I seep into the lower portion of the body.

"If you don't get out of her now I'll evaporate you."

"Oh my God," she says, "who're you talking to?"

"Your husband is a douche," I say.

"Karen. Just remain calm, okay, honey? Get out of there, you little shit."

"I'M FREAKING out! Baby, please tell me it's going to be . . . I think I'm losing my mind."

"Please. Don't do this. Get out of her before she gets hurt. You're going to kill her. Please trust me on this."

"I'm not leaving until you come with me."

"I can't do that."

"Where does he want you to go, honey," the wife says through tears, "is it heaven?"

"I can't go right now," he says, "I have a screen test tomorrow morning with an indie director who happens to be *really* hot these days."

"What the fuck is a screen test?"

I contract further inside her. It feels really warm, it feels incredible, actually—I don't want to leave. Is this the real earthling love? Wait, isn't this where earthling babies live? It's . . . it's absolutely amazing.

"All right," he says, "I'll do it."

"Do what?" Karen says, panting now, "do what? Hon, something's inside me, what is it?"

She falls to the floor.

"Promise," I say to the douche.

"Who's talking? What's in me? Am I dead—please, I don't like this."

He waits a long time before saying, "Promise."

I slip out between her legs.

At first she screams, and then she makes a strange sound. The electric shock must be hurting her. But it sounds like she's enjoying it. Weird.

Free from Karen's body.

Meanwhile, douche has escaped his suit; he's hovering over Karen. "What is that," she's saying, too busy watching us to notice the douche's suit fall to the floor, "in the air? Hon? Oh my God, it's . . . beautiful."

"It's time for you to go," I tell the douche.

"Nope," he says. And then his molecules begin to flatten as he's all, "Remember, Jack, all that you learned is false."

"You promised!"

"You're fucking with people's lives, Jack."

"Stop calling me that."

"What's that, Jack?"

"You have to lie to earthlings every day."

"Please. Earthlings are too busy lying to themselves to notice."

"I'm taking you back."

"Who's talking?" Karen says, standing up. "Earthlings? Oh, Jesus."

"You have to come back," I find myself saying, "it's only right."

"You don't know what's right—no one does."

"You think you know everything."

I rush at him and suddenly we are tangled. And I'm all fighting with all my strength and he's all overpowering me again, and Karen's all screaming, and then douche is saying, in our language, "Leave . . . me . . . *alone.*"

Karen crashes to the floor. Her mouth now all open. Her eyes all staring at the ceiling.

"She's okay—trust me," the douche says as I break free from him.

"You spoke in our language, you killed her!"

"Don't say that," he says, lowering to her body. For a moment we're both hovering over her, and then a string of his molecules lowers to her face, and he's all, "I think you're right."

"I'm sorry," I say, shrinking a little.

The douche takes the shape of a gigantic knife, and is all, "It was your fault!"

"You killed her," I say, shrinking to the size of an earthling eyeball, lowering to the floor, sensing he's coming after me.

"I had a mission," I say for some reason.

"How could you have done this to an earthling?"

"You did it!"

In a flash of blue and red mist—he's gone.

Meanwhile, Karen just lies on the floor, staring at the ceiling.

I should be chasing the douche, but I can't stop staring at these yellow bubbles growing inside her chest. Suddenly, particles—sand like and shit—rise from her body, hovering in the air for a bit and, like they're about to speak, escape through the window.

Strange.

Must focus.

Am sensing he's outside.

Drift out of the room, still holding the apprehension device. Thought: The apprehension device will work only if he's out of the suit. He's by the pool, heading for Zoë.

Fuck thinking!

I rush out there as fast as I can and when I see him I release the apprehension device—it floats toward him and . . . his web of molecules catch it.

Then a black mist forms around his being and he's all contracting into this solid, little ball. For a moment this ball just hangs there before dropping into the pool.

Zoë's all standing by the water, holding the head of my suit and saying, "Oh . . . my . . . God."

"Zoë!" I say to her.

With the sun burning the backyard, the palm trees all standing beside her, she looks so beautiful. And before I tell her so, she's all, "Clint, is that you? What am I looking at?" She's staring up at me, turning to green hands inside and saying, "You're . . . so pretty, Clinton."

I'm all, taking up space over the pool, "Zoë, something bad happened."

"Uh-huh," she's saying, looking up at me, and I'm beginning to expand so that I'm taking over the entire backyard area. "Zoë, go inside. And when you get in there, like, promise me you won't scream, okay?"

Zoë moves her head up and down, her little puddle bubbling inside her.

"Karen no longer exists, Zoë."

Zoë looks down at the head, and then up at me, and is all, "What the fuck is that supposed to mean?"

"Karen's dead."

Black and white stars begin to, like, flash inside Zoë's body . . . until this red bubble starts to grow between her breasts.

Zoë places my head on the grass.

"We'll use this," she says, and then grabs this long device from a wall and drags it along the surface of the water until the douche is safely within its net. Per my apprehension instructional, I grab the thing—it's like a pebble you'd find on the beach—reach down and use some of my molecules to lift it.

"It's weird," Zoë's saying, "to hear you speak and only see, like, you in these dots or whatever."

I'm all, hovering over the pool now, "Oh. Bring the head inside, okay? I'll follow you in there."

[pause]

When Zoë sees Karen's body, her skin turns all white, which makes her zits even redder and shit. She hands me the head portion. That red bubble has grown so large inside her I'm wondering if she's going to just fall to the ground at any moment.

Meanwhile, I place the head onto the suit, lock it, and then enter the whole thing.

"It's weird," Zoë's saying, putting her ear to Karen's chest, "I've never—"

"Seen a dead earthling?" For some reason I don't want to explain that I saw some sand stuff emerging from her body.

"You didn't—"

"He did it."

"I believe you, Clinton, I really do. Wait, how'd she, you know?"

"If an earthling hears our language, they die."

"Oh," Zoë says, gray grass all growing inside her, "that sucks."

We walk through the big room again, not saying anything, the sun all spilling through the window like this house is floating in space. Before we get outside, Zoë's red bubble has burst into these, like, gray little animals or something.

"We have to call 911, Clint."

"Who?"

"The police."

"No way!"

"This way, like, they'll come and—no wait, they'll think *we* murdered her. Quick, let's just go and we'll call from a pay phone. Hurry!" Then she opens the door to leave, and says, "No. Let's call from her cell phone. This way, they'll just show up."

She begins to walk back and forth in the big room, going grayer and grayer inside. "It's the right thing to do, Clinton. I just know it." She begins biting her fingernails. "Don't argue with me on this," she's saying, "we owe it to her, like, family and stuff—wait, you think maybe a cleaning lady will discover her or something?"

I walk up to her and grab her, pulling her close to me. I can feel her heart vibrating beneath her breasts, and I try with all my strength to meet her heart area and relax it, though I don't really know how to do this. So I'm just holding her as tight as I can, trying to not say anything, when it hits me: She won't fit into the craft. I can't bring her back. Fuck!

No time to dispose of douche's suit. Occupying his suit now, walking down driveway. Around me, palm trees reaching for space. Left my suit in car with Zoë. Karen's body in the kitchen. Inside her was an empty, brown shell. Thought: Maybe they get, like, another chance; remembering Kip having said something about his "former life." I don't know, I hope in her next life Karen doesn't marry a douche.

Climbing over translucent wall now when I remember the douche's nose. Fuck. Running back up driveway to retrieve it.

Thought: Earth is made up of millions and millions of particles of thought trapped in earthlings' heads and shit.

Wait, I'm running!

[pause]

The sun is falling, spraying palm trees and earthlings and cars and buildings with this golden layer of light that, for some reason, like, rattles my molecules inside the suit. I'm all looking at this planet like I'll never see it again. Meanwhile, Zoë and me are driving in silence, the douche's suit stuffed in the trunk.

I'm almost sure that one, it's impossible to fit Zoë into the craft; two, she can't survive dark-speed; three, she wouldn't last a day on my planet, seeing how, you know, we don't have surfaces and shit; and four, she knows all of this.

Kip's car is all roaring down the hill.

I put my earthling hand on her thigh, and she squeezes it. It's weird, 'cause, like, for the first time ever, I don't feel like babbling. Feels good not to babble, actually. In fact, I'm suddenly thinking this is going to be the new me—no more fucking babbling—when Zoë all of a sudden says, "Don't look now."

"Don't look at what?"

"At the car next to us."

"Okay."

"No," she says, a pink bubble erupting inside her, "look, but don't, like, LOOK!"

"Wait, is that earthling English?"

"It's the *real* Clint Eastwood, dummy."

I look over at this earthling with gray hair sitting in what's either a red spacecraft or a very expensive car. He must have heard what

Zoë said, 'cause he's all squinting at us with these tiny, curious eyes. Something's weirdly familiar about him. The skin on his face appears wrinkled, but in an opposite-of-a-douche sort of way. Then it hits me. It's him! The real Clint Eastwood, the earthling I'm designed after! He really is just like my earthling suit, only older. "Please," I say to Zoë, having trouble turning away from him, "just go!"

"I *can't*," she says. "It's a red light."

"What if he turns me in?"

"Shh!"

Inside I'm beginning to expand and contract all bird like and shit. In fact, I'm so worried about Clint Eastwood figuring out my identity that I remove the head portion of my suit, hiding it near feet portion.

"No!" Zoë whispers so loud she's shouting, "put it back on—you're going to give him a freakin' heart attack!"

When I put the head back on, she's all, "Tell him you like his movies—that you're, like, a big fan. Just do it!"

I look over him, smile as big as I can, and say, "I'm a big fan."

He nods slow-like, this blue cube turning slowly inside of his head. His skin, meanwhile, is beginning to turn all white like Karen when she died.

We stare at each other.

Suddenly the blue cube turns into this beautiful, purple triangle that begins spinning slowly around. He is peace, I'm thinking.

Then Kip's car roars and Zoë's driving practically at dark-speed and shouting, "Oh my God, he's totally fucking following us!!!"

[resume log: 4.51]

Real Clint Eastwood didn't follow us. He just, like, turned slowly onto another street. Zoë's thought: He's probably too busy making films to bother chasing people like us. Told Zoë I'm not a people. She was all silent for a while before saying, "Right."

Thought: Actually annoyed the real Clint Eastwood didn't chase us.

Turning onto another road, we see gigantic piece of wood on which the douche's face has been placed; except his hair is all short.

Am all, "See, earthlings are all worshipping him but little do they know he's in my ass."

Zoë's silver puddle still bubbling. She's all, "Uh . . . that totally sounds gay."

"It does?"

Question: What the fuck is that supposed to mean?

[3.67]

The air is purple again, filled with pink clouds that hang over the ocean without a care in the world, it seems. Zoë's puddle overflowing, probably for Karen. Zoë and I aren't talking much. Kip's car rattling now as we park outside the house.

This mission, I'm thinking, opening the heavy door, has rearranged my molecules. For sure.

We have gone to several banks to use my nose hair to remove as much money as I can so that Zoë can, like, have money to help her mother and shit. I carry douche's suit into the house—up the stairs, where I drop it onto the bed.

His famous face is all buried into the pillow now, his arms and legs all spread out.

"Wow," Zoë says.

Am all, "Okay, maybe you shouldn't see this."

"I'm not going anywhere, Clint."

Zoë sits on floor. Then lies on floor. Then, like, curls up so that she resembles a ball. Inside her the silver puddle is beginning to swell and then it, like, explodes, all this liquid shooting up into the top portion of her body. I can't stop looking at it.

There's not much time before the douche exits my sphincter, but I just don't want to say this right now; don't want to, like, interrupt her sadness. Per instructional, reaching into the douche's nostril, digging finger portion in there as far as I can; and I'm about to tell Zoë I can't find it when I see inside her what appears to be a lemon growing in her gray puddle. Is that hope? Actually, don't give a fuck; going to think it is, anyway.

Found it! Press it. Wait it.

The douche's suit contracts so quickly it . . . disappears. What's left is a red-and-blue-colored thing the size of an earthling fist.

Zoë's crying now so hard her body is shaking. I take a seat on the floor by her. I lay a hand on her hair portion. I don't know why, but I send a little electric shock to her face. Her body rattles.

[2.99]

Per instructional, place what's left of douche's suit in the place of fire, and then strike some matches—it takes me a while to figure out—until flames erupt.

Return to bedroom upstairs. Lights off. Shadows of palm trees across the walls and shit. Zoë lying on the bed, still curled into ball, her silver pond overflowing, only that yellow thing has formed into what looks like a plant.

"Zoë."

"What?" she says in a deeper voice.

"I have to go."

"I thought," she says, turning over, her face all soaked from tears, "I was going with you."

"I'm sorry."

She rolls over so that she's staring at the palm tree shadows on the wall.

Am suddenly struck with a idea!

An idea that will totally make her feel better about us not going back together and shit. "Zoë," I say, expanding inside, all excited and shit, "I should leave you something to, like, remember me by."

Zoë lies there for a while before saying, "I'd like that."

I'm all reaching into my jeans, feeling around for indentation. Find it. Press it. Remove penis. Am holding it, the thing bouncing a little when Zoë's all staring away and saying, "Can I be totally honest with you, Clinton? Like, I never thought I could go back with you. Or maybe I'm not sure I want to. I mean, I'm sure it'd be exciting and I'd love to just, like, see you every day and spend time together on your planet, but I think—you know, my home is on Earth."

I quickly replace the penis. And am locking it as every single one of my molecules shrinks from sadness. Meanwhile, Zoë's all wiping tears from her face. "Clint?"

"Yes?"

"Can you just hold me for a little while? Do you have time for that?"

[pause]
Zoë has fallen asleep in my arms. When she sleeps, this solid, pink bar occupies her body, expanding and contracting so slowly it's actually, like, difficult to detect its movement. It's very relax-

ing. In fact, I want to lie next to this pink bar forever. But I have to go, all 'cause of this mission. As I lay next to her I'm experiencing two thoughts at the same time—or maybe it's like two roads of thoughts, each one heading in the same direction but, like, never intersecting. Sounds all douchey to me, but that's how it is. Like, sadness for leaving and joy for having accomplished the mission when Father or the committee or the scientists or anybeing never, like, taught me how to do it. Sadness and strength. Strange.

Uh-oh.

Receiving message!

So I don't wake her, I let Zoë slowly fall off me.

Then quickly climb the steps to the roof and open the door and suddenly am staring up at the stars that're all vibrating against the black sky.

[resume log: 1.89]

"ARE YOU UPSET I IGNORED YOU?"

"Father," I think in my language, "please refer to my log for status of mission."

"WHAT IS THAT SUPPOSED TO MEAN?"

"Wait, that's what I say all the time, except I, you know . . . swear."

"I BELIEVE ON EARTH IT IS WHAT THEY REFER TO AS A JOKE."

"Yes!"

"I AM VERY PROUD OF YOUR BRAVERY FOR COMPLETING THE MISSION."

"Why'd you ignore me?"

"I WANTED YOU TO LEARN ON YOUR OWN."

"An earthling died 'cause of me."

"ACCORDING TO OUR ANALYSIS, DEATH ON EARTH IS VERY COMMON."

"I guess."

"IF YOU TAKE RESPONSIBILITY FOR ALL THE DEATHS ON THAT PLANET AT ONCE, WHERE WOULD YOU END UP?"

"True."

"YOUR MISSION WILL LIVE WITH YOU UNTIL YOU EVAPO-RATE. IT HAS BECOME YOU."

That sounds a little douchey, but of course I won't tell him that.

"THE EARTH IS A YOUNG PLANET; IT HAS A LOT TO LEARN."

"But they have love here."

"OUR LOVE IS SIMPLY MORE EVOLVED."

"Evolving is boring, Father."

"AH, I SENSE YOU ARE GOING TO BE WISE LIKE YOUR MOTHER."

"Can't we help them?" I think, staring at the stars. "Their planet is, like, warming. There are too many earthlings. All they care about is winning. Their cars cough all these toxins into the air. And they talk about God and stuff, but, like . . . stores are their churches, Father."

"I DON'T SEE WHAT THEY'D GAIN BY OUR ASSISTANCE."

"Helping would, like, you know—help!"

"LIKE YOU, SON, THEY ARE YOUNG. GIVE THEM TIME."

Am thinking of Zoë now. She's sleeping on the bed, her hair the color of sand, her pretty zits. "I don't know, I still don't think I experienced earthling love, Father. Maybe I did, I don't know, or, like, I think I came close."

"PERHAPS THAT'S AS CLOSE AS ANY EARTHLING GETS."

[pause]

Return to the room to find that pink bar inside of Zoë shrinking until it's this lone wire, which begins to blink from pink to black, and then disappear. And then Zoë's silver pond appears, and she's all moving her arms in a strange way, "Clint."

"Yes?"

"You're still here? Good."

She grabs my hand as we walk downstairs, where it's all dark.

"What the fuck is burning, man?"

"Kip?" Zoë says, turning on the lights downstairs. "Kip, where are you? Are you alive?"

"Don't think so, man."

"Kip, Clint's leaving—did you hear what I said? He has to go."

"Peace out, little brother."

We find Kip lying behind the couch, his arms folded over his chest. He has these purple rings around his eyes. I'm all, "Bye, Kip."

"You going back to your planet?"

Uh-oh.

Zoë's eyes grow all big as she stares at me. "Good-bye," I say again, 'cause I don't know what else to say. Good-byes suck!

"Keep it real, brother," he says, staring at the wall.

"Uh, Kip," Zoë says, "you probably shouldn't drive your car for a while—the cops might be looking for it."

"It ain't registered, anyway, man."

Meanwhile, his body is filled with so much yellow liquid running through his veins that I wonder if he's going to live. I want to say something, like, important, something to, like, save him, but I don't know what that is, and I'm expanding inside the suit at the frustration. "Be good," I find myself saying, "to yourself, Kip."

"Ride the wave of capitalism, brother—before that shit rides you."

24

I tell Zoë we have to run, or at least walk really, really fast,
'cause I don't have much time. "Okay," she says, "let me just do the
dishes first." "No," I say, "we have to go." There isn't much time
before the douche could escape my sphincter. Truth is, I want to at
least sit with Zoë on the beach for a while before I return. Like, I'm
so fucking sad I don't want to leave. Two thoughts at once. Sucks.

Meanwhile, tiny gray bubbles of water, like molecules, have
occupied the air.

The homefree earthlings I gave so much money to are still living
on the beach. An earthling walks out of his camper, and then uri-
nates onto the pavement. "What happened?" I say to Zoë as we're
walking all fast and shit along the paved path that, during the day,
all kinds of earthlings travel with their wheeled vehicles. "Like, it's
no different than when I first showed up."

"I'm so sorry, Clint."

"I shouldn't have done that. Money is bad, right?"

"It's the root of all evil. For sure."

"Wow, that's a very, like, smart thing to say."

"I didn't make that up," she says, smiling and walking fast, "it's, like, a cliché."

"What the fuck is a cliché?"

"Tell you what," Zoë says, moving her hand now through my hair portion, "when you return, I'll tell you—how's that sound?"

"Sounds great!"

"My man."

Carl is wearing what looks like something the douche would wear, black pants and a clean, white shirt. He's standing next to another black earthling who's older than Zoë and me but not as old as Carl.

I'm all, stopping, "Hello, Carl."

Carl's all green fur inside as he smiles bigger than any earthling I've ever seen, his teeth still not white but not as dark as urine. "Been meaning to thank your ass."

"For what?"

"Your kindness."

"Kindness."

"This is my nephew."

According to the colloquilator, a "nephew" is *a son of one's brother or sister*.

"Ah," I say, smiling 'cause I'm about to say something really fucking smart, "the son of your brother or sister."

"This is the angel I was telling you about," Carl says to the nephew.

"Huh," says the nephew as these green dots begin to blink inside him.

"He helped me pay for my medication," Carl says to the nephew. "He saved my life."

I'm all, thinking about Kip and saying, "You helped saved you, Carl."

Carl just laughs, and the nephew starts smiling, then stops smiling, and meanwhile Zoë's pulling on the shirt portion of my suit.

"Uh," Zoë says, "he has a plane to catch."

"God calling you back?" Carl says.

We hurry along the sand toward the black ocean that's all roaring and shit. I say to Zoë, "Carl thinks I'm an angel."

"I can see that," she says, "you gave away everything you had."

For some reason I'm all wearing a smile that, I'm sure, if any earthling were to walk by he or she would say it sparkled.

[resume log: 00.73]

Black waves falling over and breaking apart and spilling toward Zoë and me.

Thought: There isn't much time left.

[pause]

The waves were clawing at the earth while Zoë leaned down to remove her sandals; her toes all painted green. Meanwhile, the moon had completely vanished, and the water was blacker than I'd ever seen it. Zoë put her hands in her pockets and used one of her feet to touch the feet portion of my suit. Inside her this pink flower began to erupt when she said, "So, you have everything you need?"

"Yes," I said, trying to make her laugh, "the douche is in my ass."

"I still think that's, like, totally gay."

"Fuck!"

"It's okay," Zoë laughed, and then the pink flower melted a little into her silver pond, and I was about to tell her not to be sad when it burst into these green bubbles and she was all, touching my arm portion, "Don't be afraid, Clinton."

"Duh."

"Oh, like you're not afraid right now?"

"Uh," I said, "maybe. Actually. Yes."

"Me too."

"I'm sad."

"Me too."

"I'm a douche."

"Me too."

And Zoë and me were all laughing now as the water suddenly swallowed our feet, like it was mad we were ignoring it. "Ah," Zoë laughed, "cold." Then she stopped laughing as she ran away from the water and onto the dry sand.

"I don't know what cold feels like," I said, but she didn't hear me. Then she walked up to me and grabbed my hands portions and said, "You're a nut."

"I thought I was a bird."

"You're a nutty bird."

Suddenly I was remembering what the douche had called pretty females, and so I said, "You're a bee."

"Oh, Clinton," she said, "you're so charming."

"Wait, I think I meant honey."

She took a seat onto the sand, and held her knees all close to her breast, the wind blowing her hair so that it was all covering her face. I sat down next to her and touched her pretty zits on her face, and didn't babble anything, 'cause, you know, babbling can ruin things. "You're going," I found myself babbling anyway, "to probably experience, like, lots of deaths down here, Zoë."

Zoë sat there in silence before saying, "Like, maybe it's just all this stuff with you that's happened lately, but—I swear, seeing Karen all dead wasn't that bad, you know? I mean, it's totally fucking sad, but—I don't know. You know what I mean?"

I know, I felt like saying, but for some reason I didn't. I just sat there, staring at the waves crashing and thinking of Karen, her red hair and shit. And the douche. And maybe he did treat her not all that bad, I was thinking. And all of a sudden my molecules begin to fall toward the bottom of my suit, and I was trying to gather strength to fill the suit, but really, I was crying. And feeling stupid 'cause of it. And trying to stop when Zoë said, "What's wrong?"

"Nothing."

"You sure?"

"Totally."

"Positive?"

"Maybe it's the douche," I lied, "trying to get out."

"He is?"

"No."

"Are you crying, Clint?"

I started rattling with laughter, feeling all stupid as I said, "Yes."

Zoë's face got all wet with tears. "Wait," I said, "how'd you know I was crying?"

"Just a hunch."

A green light ignited behind her eyes as she looked at me. Then she grabbed me, and we fell back onto the sand. "I'm going to miss the fuck out of you, Clinton."

"Really?"

"Totally."

"Good-byes suck."

"Oh my God. Completely."

Her molecules were vibrating against mine when suddenly I remembered my thoughts. "My thoughts!" I said.

"Uh-oh," Zoë said, "here we go again."

"What, you think that's stupid?"

"No, not at all. I was just kidding."

"Yeah, right."

"No. Come on. Please. Tell me."

"No." I crawled out from under her and, like, stood up.

"Clint, you tell me right now what you're thinking or else . . ."

"Else what?"

"I won't kiss you good-bye."

"Like . . . I'll always have you in my thoughts and shit."

"Aw, that's sweet."

"Zoë," I said, like, suddenly expanding inside the suit, "whatever you do on Earth: Don't try to *win*."

"You think?"

"Like the earth," I found myself saying, the waves roaring behind me, "it's round, Zoë! You have to be *round*."

"You are a fucking nut." She laughed. "You know that?"

"I think I have love for you, Zoë."

She stood up, and then reached to kiss my lips. I felt her tongue, and inside all my molecules were quivering. She was all, whispering into my neck portion, "I love you."

It was hard to walk 'cause my molecules were all floating in the feet portion of the suit, so I was walking like an earthling who's had too much alcohol when Zoë said, "Wait," and pulled a pen from her pocket, and then wrote something on a piece of paper.

"What the fuck is that?"

"It's my MySpace page," she said. "Look me up sometime."

I placed the paper in my sphincter in order to protect it, and started walking into the water, like, afraid to look back at her. I don't know why, maybe I was all worried if I saw her I wouldn't want to leave. Like, if I saw her once more my molecules would fall again and I'd cry like a total douche. Meanwhile, the water began to swallow my legs portion, the black ocean moaning louder and louder. Fuck fear, I thought. And I turned around. And Zoë stood there with her hands in her pockets. Her sandy hair. Her little breasts. Her earthling legs. She started waving and smiling. And so I did the same, except, you know, without the breasts part. Anyway, I started waving and smiling and I was all quivering inside when this gigantic, wet tongue slapped me and I was all falling forward. And just before I had a chance to stand to see Zoë again the ocean sucked me into its belly. And I was all spinning around in the wet darkness, all worried the capsule wouldn't find me and shit; and I'd end up, like, evaporating in the middle of the ocean. And the douche would escape my sphincter and steal my suit and swim back to the Los Angeles sector and appear in some movies, and my being inside began to contract into the size of an earthling eye and once again I found myself remembering "my thoughts" and so I thought that I had to stop fucking thinking and—just ... let ... go.

ABOUT THE AUTHOR

Tom Lombardi's writing has appeared in the *New York Times Magazine*, *McSweeney's*, *Fence*, *Nerve*, and others. He currently lives in the Los Angeles sector of the vast land whose states are all united. For more information, visit his website: www.tomlombardi.org.